Ken Bruen ⁝ ·

hails from the west of Ireland and divides his time between Galway and south London. His past includes drunken brawls in Vietnam, a stretch of four months in a South American gaol, a PhD in metaphysics and seven of the most acclaimed crime novels of the decade.

The McDead is the third instalment in his land-mark WHITE TRILOGY, following on from *A White Arrest* and *Taming The Alien*.

The McDead

Ken Bruen

BLOODLINES

First Published in Great Britain in 2000 by
The Do-Not Press Ltd
16 The Woodlands
London SE13 6TY
www.thedonotpress.co.uk
email: thedonotpress@zoo.co.uk

C-format paperback: ISBN 1 899344 60 8
Casebound edition: ISBN 1 899 344 61 6

British Library Cataloguing in Publication Data. A catalogue
record for this book is available from the British Library.

b   d   f   h   g   e   c   a

Printed and bound in Great Britain by
The Guernsey Press Co Ltd.

For Jess

Kick off

'Am I dying?'
Answer that. Do you lie big and say, like in the movies, 'Naw, it's just a scratch,'? Or, clutch his hand real tight and say, 'I ain't letting you go, bro','?

Chief Inspector Roberts was a professional; a professional liar, among other things. It didn't teach you that in the police manual. No, that came with promotion. He considered all the lines he could use. What he said was, 'You're dying.'

Roberts had got the call at three in the morning. The hour of death. Coming reluctantly out of sleep, he muttered, 'This better be bloody good.' And heard, 'James!'

No one used his christian name, not even his wife. He said, 'Tony… Good Lord… where are you? D'ya know what time it is?' And heard a sad laugh.

Then: 'I didn't ring to ask the time. I'm hurt… I'm hurt pretty bad.'

He sounded hurt, his speech was coming through slow and laboured. Eventually, Roberts pinned down an address, said, 'Don't move, I'm on me way.'

Again, the sad laugh, 'I won't move, I can guarantee it.' Roberts dressed quickly. His wife was asleep in another room. Yeah, like that.

'Would it fuck.' Roberts said aloud, 'God, I haven't much called on you… I know… but maybe this would be a good place to start.'

He'd learned from his sergeant, a dubious example of catholicism, that it was a bartering thing. You did something for God, He did something for you. Like the Masons really.

He wasn't sure what he had to trade and said, 'I'll… ah… do good works.' What that entailed he'd no idea. Perhaps buy *The Big Issue* more regularly and not wait for change.

Yeah, it was a place to start. He waited, then tried the ignition again.

Nope

Nada

Zilch

He glanced briefly upwards, said:

'It's about what I figured.'

A mini-cab later and he arrived in Stockwell, where the pitbulls travelled in twos. Ludlow Road is near the tube station, a short mugging away. At that hour the streets were littered with

the undead,

the lost, and

the frozen.

8

The building was a warren of bedsits. No lock on the front door. A wino was spread in the hall, his head came up wheezed: 'Is it Tuesday?'

'No.'

'Are you sure?'

Roberts wondered if the guy even knew the year but hey... he was going to argue? He said, 'It's Thursday... OK?'

'Ah, good. I play golf on Tuesdays.'

Of course.

Flat six had a cleaner door than most. It was ajar. Roberts entered slowly. Entered devastation-ville. The place had been thrashed, cushions slit open, TV smashed, broken chairs and crockery, and his broken brother lying in the bathroom. He was a mess of blood and bruising. From the angle of his legs, Roberts knew they were gone. He opened his eyes, well, half opened one. The other was shut down. By a hammer it seemed.

He said, 'James, can I get you something?'

And Roberts tried not to smile, bent down said:

'I called an ambulance.'

His brother seemed to have lost consciousness, then said: 'Oh good, is it a weekender?'

A south-east London maxim. You called one on a weekday, could expect it on Saturday. Roberts didn't know what to do, said: 'I dunno what to do.'

That's when Tony asked if he was dying. He tried to cradle his brother's head, there was blood everywhere, asked, 'Who did this, Tone?'

'Tommy Logan.'

Before he could ask more, his brother convulsed, then let his head back, and died. When the medics arrived and scene of crime boyos, Roberts was led outside to the ruined sitting room. As they moved the body, a mobile fell to the floor. The officer in charge said, 'I'm sorry, guv, but I have to ask some questions, you understand.'

'Yeah.'

'Did he say anything?'

'No.'

The officer tried to proceed delicately, asked, 'He called you?'

'Yeah.'

'And he didn't give any indication of what had happened?'

'He said he was hurt and could I come.'

'Yes?'

'I came.'

'Right… was he… ah… conscious… when you got here?'

'No.'

The officer looked round, said, 'I see.' But he didn't. Went another direction, asked, 'Were you close , guv?'

'Close?'

'You know, like regular contact?'

Roberts focused, then said, 'I spoke to him ten years ago… maybe eleven.'

'Ah, so you weren't, then?'

Roberts turned his full look on the officer, said, 'No wonder you're a detective.'

Living next door to Alice

(Smokie)

W PC Falls was standing in front of the Superintendent. He was drinking tea and drinking it noisily. It's a very difficult task to chew tea but he appeared to have mastered it.

Gnaw

gnaw

gnaw

Like an anorexic rodent. He'd get it down but that didn't mean he had to like it. Worse. A biscuit, a club milk. He slid open the wrapper, then carefully peeled back the silver paper, said, 'They're well protected.'

Did he mean the public, criminals, tax dodgers? So, she

just said, 'Yes, sir.' Which is about as unthreatening an answer as you can get.

WPC Falls was black and pretty or, as they said in the canteen, 'She's pretty black'. Argue the toss. Recently, she'd fucked up spectacularly in both her personal and professional life. She'd been pregnant and had gone after an arsonist alone. Nearly killed, she'd lost the baby and almost her job.

DS Brant had forced her along to arrest a hit man. It had saved her job and restored some of her confidence. Not all, but definitely in the neighbourhood. After, he'd said, 'you know Falls, you're getting a mean look.'

'What?'

'Yeah, a nastiness around the eyes.'

She couldn't resist, said, 'Like you, sergeant?'

He laughed, answered, 'See what I mean? Yeah... like me and, if you're real smart, you'll work on it.'

Surprised, she asked, 'Will it go away?'

'Fuck no, you'll get meaner.'

The Super put the biscuit to the side, said, 'Gratification postponed is gratification doubled.'

Falls had a flurry of thoughts – *Thank Christ he didn't start on the biscuit. Yer pompous fart* – all hedging on the insubordinate. She cautioned herself. Chill to chill out. Now the prize prick was flicking through her file adding sighs, tut-tuts, teeth clicking, every few pages. Finally, he sat back, said, 'A checkered career to date.'

'Yes sir.'

Now he was tapping a pen against his teeth, exclaimed, 'And such promise, you have the potential. Oh yes.'

Falls thought, Yeah, I'm black and a woman.

He closed the file then, as if only now was the idea crystallising, said, 'I'm going to take a chance on you Falls, eh.'

'Thank you, sir.'

'No doubt you're familiar with the Clapham Rapist?'

Who wasn't? A serial, he'd attacked six women, six black women. The lefties were kicking up a stink. Phrases such as 'selective policing' were surfacing.

He continued: 'You'll be living in a bedsit in Clapham, going to pubs, clubs, all the places this johnnie hunts.'

She tried to restrain herself but couldn't, said, 'A decoy?'

He gave a tolerant smile, said, 'Not a term we're keen on my girl, smacks of entrapment. We'll have you covered all the way.' Sure. 'So, are you up to the job? I've picked you especially.'

'Yes, sir.'

Thank you sir. Won't let you down sir, etc.

Brown-nosing to screaming point.

'Good, the desk sergeant has the details. PC McDonald will be assisting you… that's all.'

She was just closing the door when he pounced on the club milk. Could hear him wolfing it as she moved away, muttered, 'Hope it bloody chokes him.'

As Brant had said, 'Getting meaner by the minute'.

The Greeks have a
word for it

There's a narrow street connecting the Walworth Road to the east entrance of The Elephant and Castle shopping centre. It has second-hand furniture shops, a bookies, a boarded-up off licence and a taverna. The taverna is called The Spirit of Athens. It's a dump. But it does OK, and has a minor reputation for its bacon sarnies. A hint of kebab is added to the mix and the locals like it. Gives a taste of the exotic and disguises the bacon.

Culinary delight indeed.

The owner is named Spiro Zacharopoulos. He's a snitch and, more to the point, he's DS Brant's snitch. Brant looked like a thug and he was real proud of that. The

Metropolitan Police *believed* he was a thug and were deeply ashamed of him. He'd had some major fuck-ups in his career which ensured he'd not rise above the rank of sergeant. But a number of last moment high profile case solutions had saved his career. It was always thus, thin ice to the promised land.

A mix of ruthlessness and the luck of the Irish kept him in the game. Snitches were the lifeblood of police work. Brant knew this better than most. Now sitting at a table, he said to Spiro, 'Jaysus, would it hurt to give the place a sweep?'

'Ah Meester Brant, help is so… how you say… diskolo… difficult to get.'

'By the look of this joint, it's downright impossible. Couldn't you get a brush?'

Spiro spoke perfect English but it was useful to play it down. Gave him the edge. He said, 'Ah Meester Brant, you make a joke.'

Brant reached into his jacket, got a pack of Weights and a battered Zippo, lit up, exhaled, said, 'When I make a joke boyo, you won't be in any doubt about it.'

Spiro, playing the anxious-to-please role, went and got an ashtray. Written along the side was Ouzo-12. Brant looked at it, flicked his ash on the floor, said, 'That's going to make all the difference, eh? What's the twelve for?'

Now Spiro could be the true Greek, hospitable friendly sly, said, 'Ouziko Dodika.'

'Which tells me what exactly? Doesn't tell me shit pal.'

'Wait… wait one moment.' He got up, crossed to the bar and busied himself. Five minutes on he's back with glasses, a bottle, snacks on plates and a jug of water, says, 'Let me demonstrate.' Pours the ouzo, adds water and it becomes the colour of window cleaner, nods to the snacks,

15

explains, 'These are meze, we eat, we drink, like we're in Greece.'

The 'snacks' consisted of

two Ritz crackers,

two slices of 'rubber',

two thin wedges of cheese.

Brant stared, then: 'Jaysus, you broke the bank with all this grub… what's the rubber bits?'

'Octopu.'

'I can only hope you're kidding. Tell you what, I'll feast on the others – you have the condoms.'

He took his glass and before he drank, Spiro said, '*Aspro pato*.'

'Whatever.' Knocked it back, gasped and said, 'Paint off a fucking gate…'

'You like?'

Brant wiped his mouth, bit on a stale cracker, said, 'Let's cut the crap, boyo, and drop the Greek lesson… OK? You came to me pal offering yer help if I could help you with some problems. I delivered, you haven't been shut down so, let's hear it. You're a snitch, so snitch.'

Now Spiro was the offended party, whined, 'Meester Brant, ah… I thought we were friends. Friends do each other a *leetle* favour.'

He was into it now and would have built to operatic outrage but Brant leant over, gave him an almighty wallop to the side of the head, said:

'You're not paying attention, Costos.'

'It's Spiro.'

'See, now you're listening. Who's the main player these days?'

The main player had been Bill Preston. He was on sabbatical and various villains were vying for position.

Spiro glanced round the empty restaurant, then said, 'Tommy Logan. Like you, he is Irish, I think, but he has the mind of a Colombian.'

'What's that mean?'

'Without mercy, no… how you say…? boundaries… is why he is top because he will do anything.'

'Well now, I'd like to meet the bold Logan.'

'Mister Brant, be careful, this man is crazy. He has no respect for police or for anybody.'

Brant poured some ouzo, said, 'Let's have some more turpentine, drink to Tommy Logan.'

'Ah, you begin to like the ouzo.'

Brant leant over and Spiro cowered, but the sergeant only put his arm round the Greek's shoulder, squeezed, said, 'I like you Costis, you and yer shit-hole caff.'

Song for Guy

A handful of mourners at Tony Roberts' funeral. The Chief Inspector, Brant, Falls, McDonald, and a wino who looked vaguely familiar, but Roberts couldn't quite recall where from.

The vicar read, 'Man is full of misery and has but a short time to live…'

Brant nudged him, none too gently, said, 'Jaysus, padre, something less depressing.'

The vicar said, 'I say, do leave this to the proper authority. There are set rules and services.'

Brant gave him the look, asked, 'Wanna be first in the hole?'

The padre looked for help but none was forthcoming, so he read an up tempo passage on light and salvation. Brant liked it fine.

A persistent drizzle was coming down, not an outright soaking but a steady wetting. As if it hadn't the balls to just pour on bloody down. When the body had been lowered, Brant moved near to Roberts, asked, 'All right, guv?'

'What… oh yes… thanks… listen, I, ahm… don't they usually have sandwiches for people after…?'

Brant smiled gently, a rare to rarest event, said, 'I put a few quid behind the bar at The Roebuck, they do a lovely spread.'

'Oh, do they?'

'Well the owner's a mick, knows about wakes. He'll do us grand. I'll leave you a moment, guv.'

Roberts turned, asked, 'What will I say? I dunno what to say.'

'Tell him goodbye, guv… oh… and that you'll fix the fuck what done him… OK?'

Only Roberts and the wino remained. Then it came to him – the wino outside Tony's door. The man said, 'Sorry for your trouble, he was a gent he was. Gave me a few quid now and again.'

Roberts reached for his wallet and the man was horrified. 'I didn't come here for beggin'.'

'I know, I appreciate that, but for a last one with… Tony… would you humour me?'

The wino was indignant but not stupid, took the cash, said, 'So long's you know I didn't come cos o' that.'

Roberts nodded, stood alone for a moment then whispered, 'Goodbye Tony, I'll fix the fuck what done you… OK, lad?'

T⦿p d⦿g

There's a new boot on the market. Heavy, thick-soled, menacing and highly impressive, called *Wehrmacht*. And, yeah, they pronounce it with a V and a tone. So, OK, it's not actually called the Third Reich, but it's implied. Could they give a fuck. Selling like designer sunglasses. Tommy Logan had a pair and he adored them. For good measure, he had the toes reinforced with steel. Kept them spit-shined and did those mothers gleam?

His real name was Tommy Nash but that was before. In the Scrubs, he'd drowned a guy in a toilet. Not an easy task. You have to truly want to kill somebody. Tommy did.

That evening in the recreation room, Johnny Logan won the Eurovision for the third time. The cons were allowed to watch. To be in the Eurovision three times is some awful sentence but to win it three times, that's diabolical. One of the lifers said, 'Hey Tommy, you know what?'

'Yeah?' Lots of hard in his answer fresh from the afternoon kill, he was bullet-proof.

'You look like that guy – that winner.'

Tommy checked round, see if it was a piss-take. No. Lots of con heads nodding. Yeah, they could see it. Tommy heard the word WINNER. It sang to him.

Johnny Logan was tall, dark hair, and the face of a cherub. He sang like a tenor angel. Tommy was short with mousy hair and a baby face. But the fit was in.

Next day Tommy got a prison make-over. Had one of the cissies dye his hair black using polish and gel. Got it sleek and raven. After, he let the cissy go down and came quickly. A few minutes later he beat the cissy to pulp, shouting, 'I hate fucking queers, man I just fucking hate 'em.'

On Tommy's release he didn't go back to north London. He headed south-east and became Tommy Logan, adopted a half-assed Irish accent and thought it passed for humour. To complete the transition, he got a heavy gold Claddagh ring and ordered bottles of Guinness in public. It worked for Daniel Day Lewis. His music of choice was Sinead O'Connor. He believed her to be openly psychotic. Her songs sang to him of

violence

pay-back

fuck you-all.

The current favourite was Troy, where her Dublin accent lashed full and lethal. Jaysus, he couldn't get enough of it. To hear Tommy sing the chorus with Sinead was to understand Armageddon. When she grew her hair again, he was a tad disappointed. To complete his Irish

21

accreditation, his weapon of choice was a hurley. The national sport in Ireland, apart from talking, is hurling. A cross between hockey and homicide.

A hurley is made from ash and about the length of a baseball bat. Twice as lethal as it's much handier to swing. You get one in your hands, you want to swing like a lunatic.

Every year the All Ireland Final was broadcast to London and Tommy relished every murderous minute. He'd spotted a poster of the Mayo team at an Irish dance and had it away. The team looked like a hardened bunch. Tommy imagined getting them behind you in the yard at Wormwood Scrubs and shouting 'Up yah, boy.'

Jeez, what a rush. During the televised final, regardless of who the teams actually were, Tommy would shout, 'C'mon Mayo'.

While this would have been much appreciated in Mayo, it tended to confuse elsewhere. Tommy made his pile with crack cocaine. Got right into the very bases and wielded intimidation from the off. Knowing no limits, he grew into major league.

Bill Preston had been top of the south-east for a decade and when he took off, Tommy was next in line. His motto was:

The only good witness is a dead witness.

And his lack of jail time proved it. On the climb up, Tommy learned about care, caution, planning, and the best solicitors.

Front everything.

Hide

Hide

Hide

Start a company daily and muddle your tracks. A high

profile led to heat and Tommy was beginning to appreciate the value of stealth. His one major weakness was his
temper. He hadn't yet learned to control it. Tony Roberts
was proof of that.

Wake up

The Roebuck had, as Brant predicted, laid on a 'grand spread'. Mountains of sandwiches. Cocktail sausages, nicely burnt. Lashings of tea, soup and, of course, plenty of booze.

Roberts was holding a cup of tea; he hadn't tasted it. Falls prepared a plate of food, brought it over. He shook his head, she urged, 'They're very good, sir, try one of those lads.'

'No… thank you.'

Brant came over, nodded to Falls, and she backed off. Brant took the tea from Roberts, put a glass there instead, said, 'It's Irish, kick like a bastard.'

'OK, Tom.'

The others looked round.

Tom!

It never occurred to them Brant had a Christian name. His expression told them they best forget it. PC McDonald was a tall blond Scot. Falls might have felt an attraction if he wasn't so… smug. He was wolfing down food and she asked, 'Missed breakfast?'

He gave her a glorious smile. It was a winner, he'd been told and often made women weak at the knees. She said, 'You're the rising star.'

Now he was modest, toned down the smile wattage, said, 'I got lucky.'

'Word has it you'll get Brant's stripes.'

'Oh I dunno, would I be up to his rep'?'

Now Falls treated him to *her* smile. All teeth and absolutely no warmth, said, 'You've got that right.'

He grabbed a napkin, carefully wiped his mouth, and she thought, Uh-oh, all the moves.

He touched her arm, said, 'When we're done here, I wonder would you like to come back to my place?'

'When we're *done* here – you mean scoffed the food, then we'll scarper?' He decided to play, prove he could be a fun guy, said, 'Yeah… sound good?'

She moved his hand away, asked, 'And back there we'd do what exactly?' The full smile now.

'Oh, something will come up, eh?'

She looked full at his crotch, said, 'If we waited for that to come up, we'd be here all week.' And moved away.

McDonald considered following but then grabbed another sandwich, muttered, 'Cold cunt.'

Brant and Roberts had moved to a table, a line of empty shot glasses on the counter. Roberts said, 'God, that's a strong drink.'

'Aye, takes the edge off.'

They laughed at that notion. The drink hasn't been

invented that *keeps* the edge off. Still, they'd enjoy the reprise.

Brant asked, 'What the medical examiner say, guv?'

Roberts had to shake himself, focus on where he was, said, 'That he'd been beaten with a stick… maybe a club, broke every bone in his body. A systematic beating was how he described it. Took a while. Took a while.'

They digested that, then Roberts asked, 'What d'ya think, a baseball job?'

'Could be a hurley, guv.'

Roberts nodded, then, 'I know who did it.'

'Jesus, guv, are you serious?'

'Tony told me before he died.'

'And you haven't told anybody.'

Roberts raised an eyebrow, said, 'I'm telling you.' And he did.

When he was finished, Brant whistled, said, 'This is what they call synchronicity, I think.'

'What?'

'Sting had a song about it… well he would, wouldn't he? You know, like coincidence.'

Roberts was lost, said, 'I'm lost.'

Brant was almost excited. 'Guv, I've a new informant and guess who he says is the new kid on the block?'

Now Roberts gave a bleak smile. 'Mr Logan?'

'Bingo!'

Roberts stood up, swayed and Brant asked, 'We're going to get him now?'

'Oh no, that's something I want to do properly. I want to savour it. I'm going to get some more of that Irish.'

Brant sat back, said, 'That's the spirit, guv.'

Private investigation

Rosie, a WPC, was Falls' best friend. When she heard of Falls' new assignment, she snorted:

'They had me on that.'

'What?' Rosie laughed.

'Did the Super tell you he'd picked you specially.'

Falls was mortified, considered lying but thought, What the hell? Said, 'Yeah, he gave me that whole crock.'

'Set you up in Clapham?'

'Uh-oh.'

'Girl, they're shitting you, when there were three victims, they weren't sure he specifically targeted black women, so they put my white ass on the line. I hung out in clubs, pubs till my Jack said he'd get a divorce.'

'Did you talk to the victims?'

'Honey, they're black... are they gonna open up to a

white girl – a white *po-lees* girl? Sure, where you been girl?'

As she spoke, she realised, and tried to counter, 'Oh gawd, I mean… I'm a stupid cow, I'm sorry.'

'It's OK. Anything else?'

'Well, they got in a profiler… just like the telly. He said the attacker was a white male in his thirties and that the violence would escalate. It has. He used the knife last time almost as if he were working up to a kill.'

She shuddered and said, 'Don't do it girl, say you're not completely recovered.'

Falls gave her the look and Rosie said, 'Please be extra careful.'

'I will, I promise, so there.'

'You know that rape is about hate, not sex.'

'I read the report.'

'Oh… and here's you lettin' me prattle on. Then you know about the garlic.'

'What?'

'All the victims mentioned his breath stank of it.'

'Gee, that should narrow it down. We can eliminate all young males with fresh breath.'

'Of which, in the whole of London, there's probably five.'

'Five percent?'

'No, just five.'

Falls thought about Brant, then asked, 'Do I look different to you Rosie?'

'You mean… since?'

'Yeah.'

'A little quieter.'

'Do I look… mean?'

Rosie hugged her, said, 'You always looked mean.'

Lodged

McDonald was summoned to the Super's office. When he got inside, the Super came to shake his hand, did the Masonic bit. The Super sat and said, 'Take a pew son.'

'Thank you, sir.'

'You set for bigger things?'

'Yes, sir.'

'But we must be seen to go through the motions. Are you with me?'

'Absolutely, sir, one hundred per cent.'

'That's the ticket. Did you know Scots are the back-bone of the force?'

He didn't, said, 'No, sir.'

'Oh yes. Now the Irish are… what's the word, too…'

'Rough?'

'Well yes, actually I was going to say Celtic.'

Time for some brass humour. He said, 'Naturally you'd be a Rangers man.'

'Rugby League, sir.'

And they took a moment to savour their wee pleasantries. Then, 'You'll be watching out for the black woman, when she's on decoy.'

'Of course, sir.'

'No need to over-do it, we don't expect a result. Keep her outta mischief eh?'

'Very good, sir.'

Now, time for the real bones. The Super leant over the desk, said, 'DS Brant continues to be an embarrassment.'

McDonald waited.

'If you were to perhaps, notice some infringement… you'd be doing your duty to… let me know.'

'I'd be honoured, sir.'

'Good man, capital… see you anon.'

When McDonald got outside, he took a moment to gather himself. Near jumped when a finger touched his shoulder.

Brant. Who said, 'Bit edgy boyo.'

Edgy, he was stunned, tried to recover, said feebly, 'Oh you know how it is when you get a roasting.'

Brant was eyeballing him, said, 'Oh? Got a bollockin' did ya?'

'Yes, sarge… yes I did.'

Brant slapped him on the shoulder, said, 'Well, keep you outta mischief.'

'What?'

'Good man, capital, see you anon.'

Check up

Roberts had been diagnosed with skin cancer. For eighteen months, he'd undergone radiation therapy. The treatment left him bone weary and with a mega thirst. Being a policeman had the same effect. Now, he was in the doctor's surgery awaiting results of a check-up.

The doctor was at his desk doing medical stuff and looking grim. Which told him zilch. Finally, the doctor asked, 'Do you smoke?'

'What?'

'It's not a difficult question.'

Roberts thought, Oh ch-err-ist, what have I now?

'No I don't.'

'Good man. Don't start.'

'What?'

The doctor smiled, not a pretty sight, said, 'Though on this occasion, you might indulge in a small celebratory cigar.'

'I'm OK?'

'Yes, you are and, with care, there's no reason you shouldn't live another six months.'

When he saw Roberts face, he said, 'Just kidding, a little medical levity. How often do I get to deliver good news?'

Roberts couldn't quite take it in, had lived with bad luck, bad news, for so long, asked again, 'And I'm OK?'

'Just stay outta the sun.'

'In England… a tall order.' Now they both laughed. A weather joke always broke the ice.

On his way out, Roberts said, 'Thank you. I'll do my damnest now to stop the malpractice suit.'

'What?'

'Just kidding, doc.'

After Roberts had left, the doctor lit a cigarette and hoped to hell it was a joke. You never could tell with cops.

Roberts said to Brant, 'Let me get those, I'd some good news today.'

'Sure thing, guv, though I'd 'ave 'ad a sarnie if I'd known you were paying.'

Roberts took the drinks, said, 'Good news, not magnificent news.'

Brant looked longingly at the food cabinet, said, 'They sure are tempting.'

They took a corner table at the back of the pub. A police position, to see and not be seen.

Brant said, 'Your boy, the Scot, is hoping to shaft me.'

'McDonald?'

'Yeah, him.'

'You're getting paranoid, Sarge, he's all right.'

'I heard the Super tell him.'

Roberts took a sip, then, 'Oh sure what did you do… bug his office?'

'Yes.'

It took a moment to sink in. Then incredulity, 'No… not even you would be that crazy!'

'The Super says I'm too Celtic.'

Roberts took his drink in a gulp, shook his head. Brant said, 'Over on the Tottenham Court Road there's a shop called Total Surveillance. A Spy Supermarket.'

Roberts put up his hand, 'Tell me no more. Good God, they'll hang you out to dry.'

'That's what they want to do, guv, this way, I'm a jump ahead.'

'You're a flaming lunatic is what you are.'

Brant signalled to the barman. Then he roared, 'Same again… before the holidays.'

The drinks came and Brant said, 'He's paying. He's had good news.'

The barman didn't appear too pleased but said, 'How nice.'

'And I'll have one of them sarnie jobs. Pop it in the toaster, let it near burn.'

The barman said, with dripping sarcasm, 'Would there be any other jobs?'

'Naw, you're doing too much as it is.'

Roberts sulked till Brant asked, 'Wanna know what they said about you?'

'No I bloody don't.'

Then a few minutes later, 'Go on then.'

'That you're out on yer ass.'
'Never.'
'Would I lie? It's on tape.'
'Bastards, keep buggin' 'em.'

Profile

B arry Lewis was thirty-two-years-old. Tall, with a slight stoop, he had blond hair in a buzz cut. Even features that missed being good looking. He was in shape due to two sessions weekly at the gym. Barry burned with hate. He'd recently lost his job 'cooking' at McDonald's. Prior to that, he'd been with

Burger King,

Pizza Hut,

Pret a Manger.

A brief stint with British Rail was hardly worth mentioning. He never did.

All his supervisors had been black and female. Each time he'd start out well. He had it all:

Punctuality,

Cleanliness,

Friendliness.

He knew how to fit, he just didn't know how to fit continuously. Slowly, the supervisors would all begin to notice, snap, 'Wotcha always got yo' eyes on me, white boy?'

As if he'd look at the bitches. So OK, once or twice he'd sneak a peek. Imagine that black flesh under his hand, all that heat. He swore out loud: 'I never touched that cow at Burger King.'

Like that. He knew they wanted it.

Or that woman at Pizza Hut who'd asked, 'Yo Barry, nice boy like you, how come you no got yourself a girl-friend?'

Putting him down. Making him go red and howling, 'See, seed a white boy blushing.'

Packing his gear at British Rail, the knife was just lying there. It gleamed. Long black bone handle and the shining blade. Took it in his hand, it felt good. No… it felt right, and he mimicked his tormentors, said, 'Ah-rite.'

Slipped it in his jacket. He'd had no plan, no outline strategy. One evening he'd gone out, had a few beers, loosened up. A trendy pub off Clapham Common, Whitney Houston on the speakers. Jeez, he'd like to do it to her. Yeah, kick fuck outta Bobby Brown first. The woman just drifted into his line of vision.

She was with friends, head back laughing. Yeah, he saw the bitch touching the men on the knees, getting them hot. Followed her out and she said goodbye to the group. Headed off *alone* in London at night? Had to be begging for it.

Next thing he had the knife to her throat, shouting obscenities in her ear. After, he wanted to kill her. The following weeks, the need grew and he went hunting. He wasn't even sure how many. Only six had gone to the cops.

He was famous. When he read the papers and they'd said, 'Reign of Terror', he'd felt omnipotent.

Now who was staring? Who was fucking blushing, eh?

Barry liked to cook. Had an Italian recipe book and was working through it. Regardless of ingredients, he always used garlic and would laugh out loud, thinking, Keep the vamps at bay. It never failed to amuse him.

He went into the new wine bar, had a glass of white. Not bad. Then he saw her. Felt the rush, oh yeah, she was next. Fit all the points,

Pretty

Black

Confident.

It was an added high because he knew he'd kill this one. On her way out, she bumped his back and he said, 'My fault.' Falls gave him her best smile.

Rosie had answered a routine call. Disturbance on the ground floor of a high-rise. Probably nothing, but she was sent to check anyway.

All quiet when Rosie got there, she banged on the door. A young woman answered, about twenty-two, her eyes had seen it all and none of it pretty. Launched into it. 'It's Jimmy, he's back on smack, beat me when I said I'd no money.'

Rosie stepped in, asked, 'Where's Jimmy now?'

'He's nodding off in the bedroom.'

Rosie smiled, said, 'I'll have a word, eh.'

'Tell him I've no money, he won't believe me.'

Rosie went to the bedroom. The curtains were drawn

and she tried the light. Nope. A figure was hunched on the bed, long hair hanging down. Rosie said, 'Jimmy?' No response. She moved over and put out her hand to touch him.

His hand came up and he sank his teeth in her hand, bit down. Rosie heard the woman scream, 'Don't let 'im touch yah, he's got Aids.'

❖

Brant was standing at the Oval. Roberts was due to pick him up. A guy had been clocking him, sussing him out. Brant was aware without being concerned. He knew it would be a hustle, he figured he'd heard them all. Finally, the guy approached, asked, 'In the market for a good watch, mate?'

'Sure.'

The guy looked round, said, 'I'm not talking yer Bangkok monkeys. None of that rubbish. This is prime.'

'Let's have a look.'

'It's a Tag.'

When Brant didn't react, the guy said, 'Like Tag Hever, man, top of the heap.'

Brant sighed, said, 'Are you going to produce it or just keep yapping.'

Brant could see it in the guy's eyes – 'a hook... gotcha.'

Out came the watch and Brant took it, said, 'It's a fake.'

The guy was stunned. 'It's no fake.'

Then Brant took out his warrant card and the guy rolled his eyes. Taking off his own watch, Brant tried on the Tag, said, 'So's you don't go away empty handed, I'm going to give you this original.'

The guy took it said, 'It's a Lorus!'

'A real Lorus, not a copy.'

'Lorus is a piece of shit, worth a fiver tops.'

Brant said, 'Here's my lift, gotta go.'

He got in and as Roberts moved into traffic, he looked back. The guy was still staring at the Lorus.

Brant adjusted the watch and Roberts asked, 'That a Tag?'

'Yup.'

'A fake though.'

'No, it's the biz. I'm as amazed as you are.'

As they proceeded, Brant continued to sneak glances at it. He was well pleased.

Roberts said, 'Mr Logan has an office at Camberwell Green.'

'Yeah, and what's he floggin'?'

'Real estate.'

'Figures.'

They parked in Denmark Hill, walked down.

Brant said, 'Like in the movies, good cop, bad cop.'

'I hate that crap.'

'Me too... so can I be the good guy?'

The office was busy. Three phones going in the outer. A receptionist asked, 'Can I help?'

Brant showed the warrant card, said, 'We need a moment of Mr Logan's time.'

She sighed, truly pissed and said, I dunno, we're frightfully busy.'

Roberts said, 'No prob. We'll go and get *more* police and come barging back. How'd that be?'

She glared at Roberts, like she hated him, said, 'Let me see.' And strode into the back office.

Brant was looking at brochures, asked, 'You live in Dulwich, guv?'

'Yeah, me 'n' Maggie Thatcher.'

Brant looked at the prices, whistled, said, 'Jaysus, you can't be hurting.'

The receptionist came back, said, 'Mr Logan can spare you five minutes.'

Tommy rose to greet them. They both clocked the hurleys crossed above his desk. Brant flashed his card, said, 'I'm DS Brant and this is my chief inspector.'

Tommy was affable, said, 'Gentlemen… please… have a seat… some tea… coffee?'

'No thanks.'

They didn't sit. Brant asked, 'Ever know a Tony Roberts?'

Tommy put his hand to his chin, like he was trying, said, 'I remember a Tony Roberts in the early Woody Allen films.'

He pronounced it 'fill-ums' like an Irish broadcaster. Continued, 'but I think he fell out with the Woodster and ended up in one of the Poltergeist things.'

He gave a little laugh, said, 'I suppose you don't mean him eh?'

Brant smiled, said to Roberts, 'See all the stuff they learn in the nick, guv, all that time to kill?'

Tommy lost his affability. 'Was there something else?'

Roberts was about to lose it when the door burst open. A woman was shouting, 'Tommy, you asshole, you put a block on my account.' Then saw he wasn't alone, muttered, 'Oh.'

Tommy did a little bow, said, 'Gentlemen, my wife, Tina.'

She was five-foot-four-inches tall, thereabouts. A face almost too pretty. You got to thinking… What's she like when all the make-up's off? Still. A lush body and she knew it. Playing men was her best act.

40

She turned to face Roberts and went, 'Oh my-God-sweet-Jesus!'

Tommy didn't know what was happening, but it wasn't good. He said, 'So Teen, I'll catch you later, here's some cash, eh.'

Roberts played a hunch, asked, 'What is it, I remind you of someone... that it? Do I look like Tony... Tony Roberts, my brother?'

Tommy couldn't help it, said, 'Yer brother? Yah never said.'

Brant smiled.

Tina said, 'No, it's a dizzy spell. I don't know who you mean.'

Roberts pressed on. 'You know what they did to him Tina? Took a stick.'

He spun round, pointed at the hurleys, continued, 'Like one of those and systematically broke every bone in his body.'

Tina sobbed, 'Leave me alone.'

Tommy went to grab Roberts arm, shouting 'That's it.'

Roberts turned and grabbed him by the shirt, ripping buttons and pushed him over the desk, said, 'Don't put yer hands on me, yah piece of shit.'

Brant said, 'Guv.'

Roberts straightened up, took a deep breath, said, 'I'll frigging have you.'

Tommy tried to fix his suit, looked at the shirt, whined 'Yah tore it. Eighty nicker and he rips it.'

Now he spoke to Brant, 'I have juice... oh yeah... you don't mess with Tommy Logan. I have connections.'

Brant said, 'You're going to need 'em pal.'

On their departure, Roberts said to Tina, 'He's going down, be smart and don't go with him.'

Tommy slammed the door. He moved over to Tina, raising his fist, said, 'Yah stupid cow.'

The ringing of the phones in the outer office couldn't disguise the sound of the beating.

At their car, Roberts put a hand against the door, took a few deep breaths.

Brant said, 'Just one question, guv.'

'Yeah?'

'Were you the good or bad cop back there?'

Fear to fear
itself unfolding

Rosie couldn't stop sobbing. Falls had her arm round her, didn't know what to say, said, 'I dunno what to say.'

'Tell me I'll be OK.'

'You'll be OK.'

Rosie gasped, said, 'Jeez, put a bit of conviction in it. Lie to me for heaven's sake.'

'I'm a bad liar.'

Rosie held up her heavily bandaged hand, said, 'It hurts so bad.'

'Didn't they give you anything?'

'Two aspirin.'

'Oh shit.'

Rosie went quiet, said, 'He's eighteen! God, I have shoes older than him!'

'Maybe he isn't HIV.'

'It's the waiting. The doctor said it could lie dormant for years. How am I gonna tell Jack?'

'I said a dog did it. A mad dog… It was true, though, wasn't it? I won't be able to make love to Jack, I mean I couldn't.'

Falls felt lost, tried 'Maybe if a third-party told him? He's a good man, he'll support you.'

'No… later he'd start to hate me. Think I should have been more careful.'

She started to cry again.

Falls hugged her, said, 'You have to hang in here, it will be all right.'

Both wondered how on earth it could ever be that.

Evening song

Falls was on her eighth night of trawling. Jeez, she thought, this life of single bars and clubbin is boring. Every guy in south-east London with the same prized line: 'Grab yer coat, you've pulled.'

At least the women had variety – 'Lemme apply yer lip gloss' through 'Same old pricks, hon, try something feminine.' Like that. Earlier she'd vented on McDonald, 'I hope you're watching my back.'

'Don't you fret doll, you're not supposed to see me.'

'Well, I haven't, not once.'

'I'm there, count on it.' But she didn't.

Asked Brant, 'Is McDonald reliable?'

'No.'

'Sarge?'

'What?'

'Gimme some encouragement.'

He handed her a canister, said, 'Take CS gas, it's encouraging.'

'Isn't it illegal?'

'I doubt yer attacker will report it... though, nowadays...'

Brant was quiet, then asked, 'Would you carry a shooter?'

'You're joking... aren't you?' He gave her the look.

She took the CS gas.

❖

Rosie was at home. Jack was working nights. She lined up twelve sleeping pills, all in a neat line. Took another hefty swig of the rum, the litre bottle going down. She was gently singing, 'I like sailors cos sailors like rum and it sure does warm my tummy, tum, tum.'

Dressed in a worn pink dressing gown, it made her feel domestic, said, 'Now to pop two of those lads, there yah go.'

It was the best she'd felt in weeks, thought, Oh God, the note... the police hate it when there's no note.

She got one of her special notelets, a Christmas present from Falls. They had a rose motif and along the top it read 'Because Rose Cares'. She carefully cut that off. Then wrote the note quickly.

The bath was nearly full and she turned the tap off. It sure smelled wonderful. She'd put in patchouli oil and mandalay scent. The steam had obliterated the mirror. Not that she'd have looked. Considered very briefly as she popped more pills what the verdict would be. How many times had she heard 'death by misadventure'? Well, she was a Mrs... could they put Mrs Adventure.

46

She had been so careful with the pills. Christ, the last thing she wanted was to throw up. The rum she'd mixed with blackcurrant cos it was her favourite. The bottle was empty. 'Oh' she said, 'I'm a greedy guts.' No more pills either. A half remembered ditty from her childhood:

> 'Now I lay me down to sleep
> I ask The Lord
> My hair to keep.'

No, that wasn't right. She could feel her mind shutting down and took off the robe. Just before she got in the bath, she left the plastic bag on the side. The water was divine and she gave a shudder of pleasure, said, 'Please remember, don't forget.' Reached for the plastic bag, 'never leave the bathroom wet, Nor leave the soap still in the watta, That's a thing you never oughta.'

Pan back from the bathroom and there, at the door, are her fluffy slippers, Snoopy dogs on the front. Pan further back into the living room and there's the note. Reads:

> 'I'm so sorry Jack.
> I love you.'

❖

As Rose ebbed away, Falls was leaving a club in Clapham, thought, This isn't working, and walked quickly past a dark alley. Then stopped. It was a short cut but you'd never dream of taking it. Not at night. Thought, Girl, you have to start moving like a victim.

The alley looked extremely forbidding. She checked for the CS cannister in her pocket, took a deep breath, muttered, 'Oh shit, let's go.'

Turned in.

Barry Lewis had nearly given up on this one. She'd always stuck to the bright side of the street. Was about to turn for home when the victim stopped. He couldn't believe it! Was she going to risk the short cut? The endless stupidity of women! She took her time, debating. Under his breath, he urged, 'Go on, go on yah black bitch, daddy's waiting.'

It worked!

He began to quicken his pace, the adrenalin building to hyper.

Back at the club, McDonald clocked Falls leaving. He had just scored with a neat little number from Peckham and was comfortable. The girl said, 'I'd love a harvey wallbanger.'

He'd been about to leave, shrugged and figured what could five minutes hurt. Turned to the girl, his smile electric said, 'Yah go for wallbanging, eh?'

Falls was about half way down the alley when Lewis hit her. She barely heard the footsteps when a shoulder crashed into her, send her sprawling. Then he was kneeling on her back, tearing at her tights, muttering, 'Gonna give it to yah doggy-style and then I'm going to turn you over, cut yer fucking throat.'

His weight was overwhelming. Falls tried to function… where was the gas? Then the weight was gone and she heard a crash. As she turned, Brant's voice asked, 'You OK, love?'

Lewis was hunched over, groaning.

Falls got shakily to her feet, asked, 'How?'

'Gotta watch out for our own.'

'McDonald?'

48

'No doubt keeping it warm.'

Brant picked up the knife, moved over to Lewis, said, 'Let's see what we got here.'

Lewis was recovering fast, said, 'Big deal, you can't prove nothing.'

Held out his gloved hands, added, 'Can't even prove the knife is mine.'

Brant said, 'Me too.'

Showed his gloves. It confused Lewis and Falls. Brant was tapping the knife against his palm, said, 'Worst scenario, you'd get two years, be out in six months. That how you figure?'

Lewis was nodding, looking at Brant, said, 'Yeah, and then guess who I'll come looking for.'

Brant said, 'Wrong pal.'

Moved fast in front of Falls. She saw Brant's hand go out, grab Lewis, pull him forward. A grunt, then a smothered scream. Brant pulled back and Lewis was on his knees, the knife embedded. Brant walked behind him, said, 'Whoops, watch yer step,' and kicked him full in the back.

Lewis went forward.

Falls said, 'Oh sweet Jesus.'

Brant took out his Weights, lit one.

Falls noticed his hands were as steady as a rock. He bent down, checked for pulse. None.

Falls said, 'I don't believe this, you'll never get away with it.'

Footsteps and McDonald came running, stopped, tried to assess the scene, asked, 'What happened?'

Brant answered, 'It's the rapist. Fell on his knife during the struggle with Falls.'

'Is he dead?'

'As a doornail.'

Brant started to walk away, said, 'You'd better call it in, I mean you are on this case.'

McDonald turned to Falls, asked, 'Are you OK? I got delayed... I...'

She spat in his face.

Fall out

Tina Logan emerged from the hairdressers.

By sweeping her hair up and to the side, the bruising was mostly hidden. Her heart sank when she saw Roberts. He was leaning against his car.

'Go away.'

'Tina, Tina... give me five minutes.'

She pushed back her hair, said, 'Look.'

'Jesus!'

'Yeah, so please... he'll kill me.'

'I just want to know about Tony, that's all.'

She sighed, said, 'Five minutes?'

'Guaranteed, the clock's already ticking.'

Got in the car. He asked, 'Wanna go someplace, get a drink?

'No, I want to get away from you.'

Reached in her bag, took out a pack of Marlboro Lights, said, 'Jeez… Lights! If Tommy sees me, I won't be worrying about cancer. They should put a health warning on men.'

She lit up, said, 'I suppose this is a "smoke free zone"?'

'Don't worry about it.'

She gave him a full look, said, 'Oh I won't, you can be sure of that.'

Roberts had a hundred questions, didn't know where to begin.

She did: 'It was so corny. I dropped some packages and he helped me. Our eyes locked over a crushed M&S bag. I didn't tell him who I was.

'Tommy was on his way up and, being more crazy than usual, I started to meet Tony twice a week. He was gentle and where I'm coming from, that's unheard of.

'Funny too. I didn't know men could get you laughing. Then when Tommy began to suspect, I tried to call it off.

'But not really.

'I couldn't give him up. He was like… the beat of my heart. The rest you know. If your're thinking would I ever say that in a court, forget it.

'What was Tony to me? He made me feel special. Like, if I was reading *The Sun*, he wouldn't look down his nose. Oh yeah, he loved Smokie.'

'Smoking?'

She laughed, said, 'No, Smokie, a pop group from the '70s who kept on playing. Tony said they were the purest pop band… "Living Next Door To Alice"?'

Roberts shook his head and she seemed disappointed, said, 'You probably listen to classical stuff. Tony said I was his Alice… corny eh?'

She was crying now, said, 'Ah jeez, me eye make-up is

ruined. They tell you it doesn't run. Believe me, every-thing runs. Can I go?'

Roberts nodded, said, 'Tina, I'll get him.'

'You probably believe that, but I doubt if you ever will.' And she was gone.

When Falls met Brant at the station, she said, 'We have to talk.'

'Naw, I don't think so. You did all right – got a commendation. McDonald's too smart to probe. He knows *he* was lucky.'

'But it's wrong.'

'Gee, that's a pity.' And he strode off.

A few minutes later, the desk sergeant called her, said, 'Phone, down the hall.'

She picked it up, said, 'Hello?'

'It's Jack.'

'Oh Jack, I am so sorry, I…'

'Yes, undoubtedly…'

'She was my best mate, Jack.'

A pause.

'She expressed a certain fondness for you too. I would like you to do something for me.'

Perturbed by his tone, she was off balance, said, 'Anything.'

'Please inform your colleagues that we want no police at the funeral. No wreaths or vulgar flowers shaped like a helmet.'

'OK, Jack, but her friends can surely attend as private mourners, I mean…'

'I most expressly forbid it.'

'Oh… well, you're upset.'

'Don't counsel me, lassie.'

'I didn't mean…'

53

'Good day to you.' And he hung up.

Dazed, she stood with the phone in her hand, then thought, It's good, good he can focus his grief, vent it and get it out.

Then she thought, The self-righteous prick. I'll send the most vulgar display he's ever seen... Yeah, fuck you too.

Powerful

Tommy Logan had gathered his men. He began, 'Now lads…' You could cut the Irish brogue with a shillelagh. He could have been speaking Swahili for all they cared. They were on a roll and cash was steaming in. Plus, they knew he was the last man on earth to fuck with.

He continued, 'Ye'll be familiar with informants. Or snitches, as they call them in this country. It seems the police have somebody doing the dirty on us.'

Raised his voice, 'Play fair I say.'

It received the required laugh. 'So now, I'll put five large into the hand of the fellah who finds the snitch.'

An animated murmur. They liked the deal.

'OK, then… go get 'im… oh, one more thing…'

They paused.

'Be careful out there.'

More polite laughter. Ol' Tommy, he was a big kidder.

Then he got on the phone. His solicitor, chosen well.

'Harry… it's Tommy Logan.'

'Tommy how are you?'

'I've a wee bit o' bother.'

'Oh dear, maybe we can help.'

Harry was a Mason, knew where help was located.

'There's two policemen, a DI Roberts and his sergeant, a guy named Brant. They've begun to harass me, upset the missus, that sort of thing.'

'We can't have that.'

'I knew you'd understand.'

'Leave it to me Tommy, it's already being processed.'

'Thanks Harry.'

'We must have that game of golf soon.'

'Of course… ta-ra then.'

'Bye.'

Unless Tommy took his hurley to the links, there was as much chance of nine holes as Brant being promoted.

The *South London Press* had a photo of Falls on the front page and the headline:

'Shy Heroine Stops Clapham Rapist'

Shy because she refused an interview.

McDonald got a brief line as her partner. He wasn't complaining. Brant's version of the event had been accepted and if he got a little glory, all the better.

Rosie's death had prevented a deeper investigation. It was known that a keg of scandal could be opened, so the authorities let it be.

Falls tried to talk to Roberts, cornered him in the canteen. He said, 'I'm sorry about Rosie, I liked her a lot.'

'Thanks, guv.'

She indicated his cup, offered, 'More tea?'

'No, I'm about finished.' Which, roughly translated meant, 'Spit it out.'

She tried. 'It's about the rapist, sir…'

'Oh yeah. Congratulations, you did well… bloody well.'

'Sir, it's about his death.'

'Good riddance I say.'

'Sir, on moral grounds…'

He put up his hand, 'Whoa, we're coppers – morality has no place in it.'

'But, sir—'

He quoted, 'If a mere code of ethics could keep it legal, there'd be no need of us. I don't give advice but lemme say this… *Leave it alone*.'

'I don't know if I can, sir.'

He stood up, said, 'You've no choice. If there's anything to be resolved here, it's why you don't appreciate the sergeant who saved *your* life.'

Walked away.

'So he knows… God, why am I surprised?'

Roberts got the call to the Super's office. No invitation to sit down, right to it.

'You're to lay off Tommy Logan.'

'*What*?'

'There's a highly sensitive investigation underway. You'd only jeopardise months of work.'

'Are you aware that he killed my brother?'

57

'Are *you* aware I'm your superior officer and to be addressed as 'sir'?'

Roberts felt reckless, dangerously so, said, 'I don't get it, Logan's not a Mason.'

The Super was up, spitting, 'I don't think I like your inference, you'd be wise to proceed with great care.'

Roberts didn't even hear him, was trying to put it together, then, 'Wait a mo! It's his bloody solicitor, that scumbag Harry Something. Christ yeah, he's definitely in the lodge.'

'That will be all Chief Inspector. I'm going to overlook your outburst, put it down to your grief. You can go.'

Roberts pulled himself together, prepared to leave. The Super added, 'It would be a conflict of interest to have you on a family case.'

'With all due respect, that's bollocks… sir.'

Moving on

Sarah Cohen was Rosie's replacement. On her arrival at the station, the desk sergeant said, 'Cohen? A bloody Yid.' She now knew what to expect. With curly brown hair, brown eyes and a snub nose, she was half-ways pretty. Like any new person, the voice in her head roared:

Run

Get

The

Fuck

Out

Now

Before…

Burning with zeal, she had done a year of Social Science. That burnt out. On a whim, she'd applied to the police. Here she was, scared witless. The desk sergeant asked, 'What would you like to do today?'

She'd been about to respond, 'A little light traffic to start and home early.'

The desk sergeant was grinning, said, 'How does the North Peckham Estate sound?'

Sounded awful is what. Before she made a total fool of herself, a voice said, 'Lay off her, Dennis.'

Brant. He nodded at Dennis, said, 'He likes to fuck with new people. I need a WPC… let's go.' And he was already moving.

The desk sergeant offered, 'Outta the frying pan…'

Sarah had hoped for a nice cup of tea to begin. She was up all night pressing her uniform. Brant was climbing into a battered Volvo, asked, 'Wanna drive?'

'Ahm, no thank you.'

A huge smile and he said, 'I love fuckin' manners.'

Falls was getting obsessed with Brant and didn't try to fight that. It stopped her thinking of Rosie which she couldn't get a handle on.

In the pub one time, they'd all been celebrating. A little tipsy, she asked him, 'How come you've never come on to me?'

'What?'

He was mid-Cornish pasty and stared.

'You've never hit on me. All the times we've been thrown together. Am I not yer type?'

He looked at the pie, said, 'Ever notice with these things, you start off cold. Lulls you into a false sense of security and then the middle is burning, leaps to the roof of yer mouth and clings?'

60

She laughed, asked, 'Is that a metaphor?'

He dumped the remains on the floor, said, 'Naw, it's just a pasty. But naw, yer not my type.'

More bothered than she would have anticipated, she got silly, said, 'Is it a *black* thing?'

'I like black fine as long as they're bimbos.'

'Oh come on sarge, I don't buy that.'

He grabbed a pint, drank half, belched, said 'I have no problem with women talking. Hell, it punctuates the time. What I hate is women thinking they've something to say.'

She was horrified, let it show, then, 'That's the most chauvinistic thing I've ever heard.'

He drained the glass, said, 'I've got a question…'

'Go ahead.'

'When this shindig's over, will you let me jump you?'

She physically drew back. 'How *dare* you!'

'See… you're a good cop, Falls, and not bad looking. But yer not a babe. You'd want to talk after we'd done it. Me, I want me kip, so I'm off, grab a bimbo, whisper sweet shite, then wham, bam, and lock the door on yer way out.'

Then he was gone. For the first time in her life she lamented not being a babe.

Sarah Cohen and Brant pulled to a stop outside McDonald's on the Walworth Road. The radio was squawking gibberish. Brant seemed to comprehend it, said, 'We're on it.'

Turned to Sarah, said, 'It's a couple of drunks, my only suggestion is, don't get too close.'

Sarah didn't answer. She intended getting a hands-on approach from day one – being a real police person.

To the left, as you enter McDonald's, there's a children's area. With toadstools for seats and other such furnishings to put the children at ease. On the wall is a portrait of Ronald McDonald, the spit of John Gacy. Not so much a haven for little people as a creation by little-minded people. A man and a woman were holed up there, shouting obscenities and hurling burgers at the staff.

Brant said, 'Pissed as parrots.'

Sarah asked, 'What's the strategy, sir?'

'I'm gonna get some doughnuts, want one?' And he headed for the counter.

Sarah felt this was her window, began to approach the couple, said, 'I say.'

Thought – 'Oh God, I sound like a school girl. Get some street in there.'

The woman had been nodding, almost out of it, then her head snapped up, spotted Sarah, called, 'C'mere love.'

Sarah did. The woman struggled to her feet and threw up over Sarah.

Brant came with coffee and doughnuts, asked, 'Jelly or sugared?'

Took a look at her, said, 'Now, that's sick.'

Peered closer, added 'I spot pepperoni, it's a bastard to keep down, here hold these.'

Then he walked to the side, pulled the fire extinguisher from its bracket, strolled back, muttering 'Point the noozle where?' Opened it up, shouting 'Go on, get outta it.' Drenching the couple and literally spraying them to the street. A round of applause from the staff. He nodded to Sarah, said, 'That's about it I'd say.' And walked out.

Sarah followed, trying to unsuccessfully clean the uniform with wafer thin napkins. She looked at the soaked couple, asked Brant, 'Aren't we taking them in?'

'Do you want to put them in the car?'

She got in beside Brant and he said, 'Open the window love, vomit will linger.' And he put the car in gear.

Back at the station, she rushed to the bathroom, was attempting to clean up when Falls walked in. She'd heard about the black WPC, said, 'I'm new.'

'Oh really?'

She looked in the mirror, wanted to bawl. Falls looked at the soiled tunic said, 'You've already met DS Brant.'

Sarah smiled, felt it was an overture, went for it. 'I'm sorry about your friend.'

'Why… did you know her?'

'No… but…'

'Then ration your grief, you'll be getting plenty.'

Sarah couldn't help it, babbled on: 'I mean, I know I can never replace her and…'

Falls cut it short, said, 'You got that right.'

And left her.

When she emerged from the bathroom, Brant was waiting. Sarah felt she already hated him. 'There you are love, c'mon I'll get a tea.' And she warmed to him again.

In the canteen, he said, 'Get us a tea, two sugars, I'll grab a table.'

Sarah looked round, every table was vacant. She got the teas and the canteen lady said, 'You're the new girl?

Oh, Jesus.

'Never you mind, pet, the teas are on me.'

Not a grand gesture, just a moment of kindness and Sarah wanted to hug her. The woman nodded at Brant, said, 'Watch that 'un, he's an animal.'

Brought the teas over and Brant asked, 'No biccies?'

'Oh.'

'Never mind but you'll know next time. I'm partial to the club milks.'

She said, 'Could I ask you something?'

'As long as it's not for cash, it's a bit early.'

'Oh Good Lord no. It's about my predecessor.'

'Rosie?'

'Yes. I know I've no right but... what was she like?'

'A loser.'

She was shocked and maybe a tad relieved. Brant finished his tea, said, 'Yeah, she got to pull the ultimate sulk you know – na-na-na-na-na – you can't catch me, like never. Everybody gets to feel guilty and she's outta here.'

Sarah thought a defence of some calibre should be shown, said, 'But if her state of mind was disturbed?'

He stood up, his closing words, 'She was a cop, yer mind is always disturbed, otherwise we'd be social workers.'

The Super's wife was a dowager. Leastways, she looked like one. She was never young but, when she got seriously aged, she'd be Barbara Cartland, or Windsor, or both.

Her home was in Streatham Vale but she was a Belgravia wannabe and managed to mention said place in every conversation. Her car broke down near the Oval and she had to abandon it. Walking down towards the cricket ground, she was in fear of her life. Her husband *did* bring his work home.

She saw a black cab. Oh merciful God! A man stepped up beside her and grabbed her arm, pinned it under his and neatly removed her Cartier watch, shoved her back, said, 'You can 'av this piece o' shit, and slung a Lorus at her.'

Brant, on being told by Roberts, said, 'I love it.'

'The Super's on some warpath.'

'Even better, I know how to solve it.'

'You're kidding, unless…'

'What?'

'*You* mugged her!'

'Close, but no. So, who do we want to do well?'

'Let's give it to the new kid, see how she cooks.'

'The Yid it is.'

Brant caught up with Sarah later in the day. He said, 'Apprehend me.'

'What?' She hoped it wasn't sexual.

'During your training, didn't they show you how to arrest someone?'

'Yes.'

'OK, then. Picture this. I'm a suspect standing at… let's say, the Oval station… OK?'

'OK.'

'So arrest me.'

'What have you done? Oh, I'm sorry, what have you *allegedly* done.'

'For Christ's sake, what does it matter?'

'I want to be prepared.'

'Oh, I get it, you're a method police person.'

She nearly laughed but stuck to her guns… 'Sarge, it's the degree of force. I don't want to club you to the ground if it's only a parking ticket.'

Brant smiled. 'Good point, though personally I prefer the clubbing method regardless. Let's say I'm a mugger.'

'A what?'

'Christ, a bloody…' And next thing he knew he was flat on his face, his hands held behind him.

She said, 'See, I distracted you.'

'I'm impressed… where'd you learn that.'

'Girls' boarding school.'

'My favourite. You can let me up now, I think you've got the hang of it.'

Brant *was* impressed. The girl had some moves and would be worth cultivating. She and Brant drove to the Oval the next day. Parked opposite the entrance, she asked, 'Why are we here?'

'You'll see.'

After an hour, the man appeared, took up his habitual position. Brant said, 'See 'im?'

'Yes.'

'Go get him.'

'Arrest him?'

'As if you meant it.'

Brant watched her go. The kid was a definite comer and not bad looking. Nice legs. He saw her approach the man, then bingo, she had his arm behind his back, marched him to the car. Brant got the door open and pulled him in the back, said to Sarah, 'You drive.' The man was protesting… 'I didn't do nuffink… hey… wait a mo'… *I know you*!'

Brant grabbed the man's testicles, squeezed, said, 'Repeat please: *I never saw you before*.'

He repeated.

When they got to the station, Brant said to Sarah, 'When you're bookin' him, check his arms.'

'For tracks?'

'Not exactly.'

Coup

Sarah was the heroine of the hour. To such an unprecedented extent that the Super emerged from his office and addressed those gathered.

'Today we have reason to be proud. A rookie applied the tried and tested methods of policing and got a result.'

He flourished the Cartier in all its gleaming glory, continued 'If this is an indication of the standard of new blood entering the service, then I say the Met has very little reason for concern for the future.'

Cheers, congratulations, and cameraderie filled the station. Quite overcome, Sarah retreated to the ladies. Falls already there, said, 'You've arrived in style.'

'Beginner's luck.'

'Or the hand of Brant, perhaps.'

Sarah was tempted to ask, 'Touch of the sour grapes?'

Falls looked directly at Sarah, said, 'Is he fucking you?'

'My God, of course not.'

'Yeah, he's doing it to you one way or another, he puts it to everyone.'

Now Sarah went for it, 'Don't worry, no one's moving in on your manor.'

Falls laughed, 'Well, you've got spunk, I'll give you that.'

Sarah eased up, said, 'Maybe we can have a drink sometime.'

'I doubt that.'

And was gone.

Brant and Roberts were in the pub. Drinking vodka because it doesn't smell of desperation, leastways, not for a while. Roberts said, 'I've been warned off.'

'I know.'

'What?'

'I told you, I've got it taped.'

'Was it the Masons?'

'Yup.'

'Fuckers.'

'What now, guv?'

'I dunno.'

'But you're not like… giving up?'

For an answer, Roberts just looked at him and Brant said, 'Good, I'd hate to chase him on me lonesome.'

Roberts laughed. Of such moments are the best friend-ships sealed. They ordered some more vodka and Roberts said, 'Shouldn't we eat something?'

'I suppose.'

'Want something?'

'Naw.'

'Me neither.'

Let the silence build a while and allow the booze to do its number. Then Brant said, 'The woman's the key.'

'His missus?'

'Yeah, get 'im through her.'

Roberts was uneasy, said, 'I kinda like her. I wouldn't want her to get hurt.'

'There's always fall-out, guv.'

Roberts chewed on that. Then, in an exact imitation of Brant, said, 'You're right, fuck her.'

Despite the best efforts of the vodka, they didn't get any further along. Then, as is the wont of alcohol, it flipped sides and Roberts thought about Smokie, thought, At least Brant won't have heard of them either.

Aloud, he said, 'Don't suppose you've heard of Smokie?'

'The group?'

'Yeah.'

'Sure , "Living Next Door To Alice".'

'You know that, too?'

Brant looked almost happy. 'They were like a cross between the Small Faces and The Hollies. Their lead singer got killed a time back, I was sorry.'

And he looked it.

The past

Next morning, Brant was sick as forty pigs. That's real bad. Dragging himself to the shower he swore, 'Never again.'

Yeah. Fragments of the night returned.

How when the pub closed, that's when they got hungry.

Off to the Chinese where they drank bamboo wine... Could that be right?

Leaning against the toilet bowl, Brant begged, 'Please let me not have had the curry.'

As he threw up, he thought, 'Damn, I had the curry.'

Afterwards, they'd come back to Brant's place and played neo-whine songs. All the great torches. Barbara Streisand, 'You Don't Bring Me Flowers'; Celine Dion, 'Theme from Titanic'; Bonnie Tyler, 'Lost in France';

Meatloaf, 'Two Outta Three Ain't Bad'.

And if the debris in his living room was any indication, they'd drank:

Beer,

More vodka

and

Cooking sherry.

'Jaysus… please, not cooking sherry.'

Threw up again. Yup, the sherry.

Got in the shower and blitzkreiged.

Coming out he felt marginally better. Then to the living room, muttered, 'Fuck,' as he surveyed the carnage. How many cigarettes, exactly, had he smoked? Shuddered to think, and he needed one now. Took a stubbie from an ashtray, lit up.

Rough.

Once he got past the coughing jag, the bile and nausea bit, it wasn't too bad. Said aloud, 'Hey, it's not as if I *had* to have a drink.'

Got his clothes on and checked out the mirror. Mmmm… least he hadn't slept in them. Still, looked like somebody slept *on* him.

In the kitchen, made the coffee, two heaped spoons. Jolt himself into the day. Added a ton of sugar and then surveyed it, said, 'I am not, repeat not, drinking that shit,' and slung it down the sink. Then he physically shook himself and left.

A few minutes later he was back, walked across the room, picked up an open vodka bottle, chugged the final hit. Waited.

It stayed down.

He said, 'Now yer cookin.'

And went to fight the day.

71

❖

At the station, the duty sergeant said, 'A woman called you.'

'Called me what?'

'Said she was yer wife.'

Jesus!

When Brant didn't say anything, the uniformed sergeant added, 'Wanted yer number but of course I said I couldn't do that. So she gave me her number.'

Passed the piece of paper to Brant, then said, 'I didn't know you had a wife.'

'I don't.' Not any more.

Mary had left him over ten years ago. Hadn't heard a dicky-bird since.

Called the number and when a woman answered, said, 'It's Brant.'

'Oh Tom, thank you for calling me back, I wasn't sure you would.'

'What do you want?'

'No hellos or how are you?'

'You rang to see how I am?'

'Well, not completely but...'

'So get on with it.'

He heard the click of a lighter, the inhale of smoke, nearly said, 'You smoke?' But then, what was it to him? She could mainline heroin, what did he care?

Then:

'My husband, Paul... I married again five years ago... he's in trouble.'

'What kind?'

'He was accused of shoplifting at M&S, at their flag-ship store.'

72

'Their what?'

'The big one at Marble Arch.'

'What did he nick?'

'Oh Tom, he didn't... the store detective stopped him outside, said he didn't pay for a tin of beans. He'd over thirty pounds of shopping. Would he steal a tin?'

'Would he?'

'Course not. Can you help?'

'I'll try.'

'Thank you Tom, I've been so worried.'

'What's the name?'

'Silly me, it's Watson, he's the security officer on food.'

'*Your* name, your married name.'

'Oh.'

'It would be useful if I had your husband's name.'

'Johnson... Paul Johnson, he's...' Brant hung up.

What he most wanted to know was why he was so reluctant to use the word 'husband'.

Kebabed

Spiro the snitch was having a bad morning. The VAT crew had been on the phone and promised a visit soon. Plus the health inspectors he'd managed to twice defer. But, he knew he couldn't do that indefinitely. He'd have to get Brant to do it for him.

Aloud he said, 'Mallakas' – or seeing as he was born and reared in Shepherd's Bush, he could have simply said, 'Wankers'.

He had a few words of Greek but rationed them carefully. He was attempting to clean the spit for the kebab meat. Standing vertical, usually it was shrouded in meat and he carved accordingly. Now, it was bare and red hot. It gleamed with heat and hygiene. About to turn if off when there was a loud knock. A voice said, 'Police.'

'Now what?' he fumed as he went to get it.

Tommy Logan and two of his men.

Spiro said, 'You're not police.'

'We lied.'

With a dismal record in the Eurovision, the Greeks were familiar with the winners. Spiro stared at Tommy, asked, 'Are you…?'

'Trouble? Yes I am, let's take it inside.'

They bundled Spiro back into the taverna.

Tommy said, 'Spring cleaning or should that be spit cleaning?'

Spiro said, 'I'll turn it off and perhaps I can get you gentlemen a drink.'

'No, leave it on, gives the room a cosy atmosphere.'

Tommy stared at Spiro, said, 'Let's do this quick and easy. You've been telling tales to the Old Bill, haven't you? No lies or I'll make you lick the spit.'

Spiro was close to emptying his bowels, and yet his mind registered how awful a dye job Tommy had.

He put out his hands in the universal plea of surrender, said, 'On my mother's grave, I didn't.'

Tommy grabbed Spiro's hands, said, 'Hold him.'

The men did, then dragged Spiro over to the spit. Tommy said, 'You're a hands-on kind of guy, I can tell.' And slapped Spiro's hands to the hot metal.

His screams were ferocious and Tommy screamed right along with him. Then he let go and Spiro fell to the floor, whimpering.

Tommy said, 'Next it's your tongue, then yer dick. We'll kebab till the early hours. Or would you prefer to talk?'

He talked. Tommy listened, then said, 'Spiro… it is Spiro, am I right?'

Nod.

'Do you know me?'

Shake.

'So why are you making trouble? What should I do now? Do you feel up to a solid beating?'

'No… please…'

'OK.'

Spiro was too terrified to hope. Then Tommy said, 'You've cost me an arm and a leg so let's break one of each… you choose.'

It got a bit messy and they had to break both arms and his left leg.

Tommy said, 'You've a fine pair of lungs on yah.'

As they were leaving, Tommy asked one of his men, 'You eat that Greek food?'

'Me… naw, I like Chinese.'

Tommy shook his head, said, 'Irish stew is hard to top… Give the polliss a call, say their Greek takeaway is ready.'

Shopping

Brant went to 'records', gave Shelley his best smile. She wasn't buying, least not right away, said, 'You want something?'

'To take you dancing.'

'Yeah... sure.'

'Honest, the Galtimore on a Saturday night, all of Ireland and oceans of sweat and porter.'

'How could a girl resist... whatcha want?'

'A security guard with Marks and Spencer, name of Watson. He's at their flagship. You know what that is?'

'Sure, Marble Arch.'

'Jeez, everyone knows it, eh?'

'Do you want the straight CV, or do I dig?'

'Dig please.'

While he was waiting he lit a cigarette. Shelley looked

at the profusion of NO SMOKING notices but said nothing. Ten minutes later, she said, 'Gotcha.'

Got a printout, showed it to Brant. He said, 'Looks OK.'

'Take a look at 1985.'

'Ah.'

'That's it.'

'Thanks, Shelley, I'll remember you in my prayers.'

'Is that a threat or a promise?'

❖

Brant enjoyed his excursions to the West End. To be in a part of England no longer English… pity the parking was such a bitch. Finally he got a space off the Tottenham Court Road end of Oxford Street and hiked to Marble Arch. His hangover was crying out to be fed but he decided to wait. The crankiness might help his endeavour.

At the entrance to M&S was, as luck would have it, a security guard. Tan uniform, tan teeth. Brant flashed the warrant card, asked, 'Where might I find Mr Watson?'

'He'll be in the basement, foodstuffs are his manor.'

'All right is he?'

The guy looked at Brant, the look that yells, 'Do me a favour pal,' but said, 'He's a supervisor.'

'All right as a supervisor is he?'

'I couldn't say, I only know him on a professional basis.'

Brant had an overwhelming desire to kick the guy in the balls, but said, 'Don't give much away do ya, boyo?'

The guard put a hand on Brant's arm, moved him slightly to the left, said, 'You're impeding free access.'

'God forbid I should do that. Tell you what though, do you have a good friend?'

78

'What?'

'Cos if you put a hand on me again you'll need a good friend to extract it from yer hole. No carry on, no slouching.'

In the basement, Brant clocked him instantly. No uniform but eyes that never saw civilians. He was standing near the fire door. Brant let him see his approach. Nice and easy, loose, asked, 'Mr Watson?'

'Yeah.'

Oh lots of hard. This was a guy who doled *out* the shit, always. But Brant knew they were mostly cop wanna-be's, so he flashed the card, said, 'Could I have a moment of yer time?'

Deep sigh. Like, not really but for a brother in arms, only don't lean on it. Said, 'Come to my office in back.'

It was a broom closet but if he wanted to call it that, be my guest. There was one swivel chair and a small desk. He sat, put his feet up, said, 'Shoot.'

You knew he'd rehearsed it a thousand times. Brant could play, said, 'You got a guy on shoplifting a few weeks back.'

Watson sneered 'Buddy, I get hundreds every week.'

'Of course, this was literally a tin o' beans.'

Now Watson's eyes lit up, 'Yeah, he freakin' cried, can yah believe it? Big baby.'

Brant let him savour, then, 'Can you let it slide?'

Guffaw.

'In yer dreams, buddy.'

Brant was peaking, couldn't believe his good fortune. Who could have prophesied such a horse's ass? Decided to let the rope out a few more inches, said, 'As a brother officer, I'm asking for a bit o' slack. Doesn't hurt to have a friend in The Met.'

Watson was off on it, power to full octane, said, 'No way, José.'

Brant hung his head, and Watson, flying, said, 'Don't do the crime if…'

Before he could finish, Brant was roaring:

'Shudd-up, yah asshole, and get yer feet off the desk…'

Brant leant over, nose to nose, said, 'I tried to do it the easy way. But, oh no, Mister Bust-Yer-Chops gets all hot.'

Watson blustered, tried to get the reins back, 'You've got nothing on me.'

'Does M&S employ criminals?'

'What… of course not!'

Brant took the paper from his jacket, slapped it on the table, said, 'I draw yer attention to 1985.'

Watson looked, then, 'You've no right to that, it's not on my application form.'

Realising what he said, he shut down.

Brant read:

'1985 – Watson – D&D – Suspended. They see this, they'll bump yer ass from here to the dole queue.'

Watson said, 'If I could… make it right with the other thing, you'll go away?'

'Well, I'll call in now and again, see you're not slacking.'

Resigned, Watson said, 'The perp's name again?'

'Perp?'

'You know… the perpetrator…' He looked up, anxious to please, said, 'The alleged… now cleared… person's name?'

'Paul Johnson.'

Brant threw his eyes round the closet, turned to leave.

Watson offered, 'I was only doing my job.'

'Naw… you're a vicious little shit. Stay outta south-east London.'

Whining now, 'Me old Mum lives there.'

'Move her.'

Brant rang Mary, said, 'It's Brant.'

'Oh hello, Tom.'

'It's done.'

'What? Oh my God, Paul… Paul will want to thank you.'

'No need.'

'Tom, maybe we could all meet, have a meal, our treat?'

'C'mon Mary.'

'Oh.'

'Goodbye then.'

'Tom… Tom if ever we can…'

But Brant had rung off.

Mary knew she should be elated but what she felt was a sense of let-down, a whisper of sadness.

The Coroner's verdict on the Clapham Rapist was 'Accidental Death'. Falls and McDonald sat on opposite sides of the hearing. Twice he'd tried to approach her, trying, 'Can we move on?'

'No.'

Then: 'If we're going to have to work together at least…'

'Fuck off.'

He'd let it be.

In an unusual development, the Coroner praised the police for the conclusion of a fraught and dangerous episode. Falls squirmed.

Outside, she managed to dodge most of the reporters.

81

A woman came up to her and asked, 'May I shake your hand?'

'Ahm?'

She took Falls by the hand and said, 'I want to thank you for ending the nightmare. I was number six. That piece of scum, I hope he rots in hell.'

The violence of the words and the ferocity of her manner pushed Falls backwards. She tried, 'There is counselling available.'

A bitter laugh, 'Oh you were all the counselling I needed.' And then she was gone.

McDonald called, 'Yo' Sarah!'

'Yeah.'

He caught up with her, said, 'I don't think I congratulated you on yer success.'

'Thank you.'

She found it the easiest answer. She gave him a fast appraisal and thought, 'Doesn't half fancy himself.'

He held out his hand, 'I'm McDonald.'

'Weren't you the…'

'Involved in the Clapham Rapist? I played a very minor role.'

'Oh, I'm sure you're being modest.'

He gave her the full heat of his smile, turned it up to full dazzler. 'Listen, whatcha say about a drink later?'

'Ahm, I don't know…'

'Hey, no strings… we work together so it's no big deal.'

'OK… why not?'

After he walked off she felt it was a bad idea. But hey, maybe they could be mates and keep it at that. She wasn't convinced, not at all.

'What do you know
about scenery?
Or beauty? Or any of
the things
that really make life
worth living?
You're just an
Animal,
Coarse,
Muscled,
Barbaric.'

'You keep right on
talking honey.
I like the way you run
me down like that.'

Barrie Chase and Robert
Mitchum in 'Cape Fear'.

In the modern world

Roberts went into a record shop. The last record he'd bought had been by the Dave Clark Five. He was stunned by the shop. The sheer volume of the noise deafened him. Everybody looked like a drug dealer. Worse, he felt like a pensioner. Mainly he wanted to flee. But gathering his resources he marched up to a counter. An assistant, a girl who looked about twelve, said, 'Yeah.'

'Ahm… I'm looking for… a… Smokie…'

'CD or cassette?'

'I think you can take it that if the customer is over forty, it's a cassette.'

'Is it hip-hop, dance, techno…?''

'Whoa, wait a moment… they're a pop group from the '70s.'

'Then you'll want retro.'

Eventually, he was led to the cassette section and, no luck.

No Smokie.

They offered to order it, saying, 'Seventies… cool.'

He declined.

Roberts sole passion was film *noir* of the forties and fifties. Now he resolved to re-bury himself in the genre. It was what he knew.

Lesson

Brant found Sarah in the canteen. She was about to have a tea and a danish.

He said, 'Wanna see another side of policing?'

She gave the danish a look of longing.

He added, 'I mean now.'

Grabbing her bag, she got up and Brant leant across, grabbed the danish, said, 'Don't want to waste that.'

The Volvo was outside and between bites, Brant said, 'You drive.'

She got the car in gear and he said, 'St. Thomas's... mmm... this is delicious, must have been fresh in.'

Sarah was cautious in her driving, conscious of him watching.

He was.

He asked, 'What's this?'

'Excuse me?'

'Yer driving like a civilian, put the bloody pedal to the metal.'

❖

They found a space to park and walked back to the hospital. Brant said, 'I frigging hate hospitals.'

'Who are we seeing?'

'A snitch, well probably an ex-snitch.'

Sarah wasn't sure how to answer so she said, 'Oh.'

Spiro was in an open ward on the third floor. He seemed to be covered in casts and bandages. His leg was suspended.

When he saw Brant, his eyes went huge with fear.

Brant smiled, said, 'Spiro!'

Spiro's eyes darted to Sarah and Brant said, 'It's OK, she's a good 'un.'

He took a long look at the injuries, then asked, 'Who did it?'

'I dunno Mr Brant, I was attacked from behind.'

'Sure you were.'

Spiro's eyes pleaded to Sarah and he said, 'I am very tired, I must sleep.'

Brant moved closer, said, 'I don't need you to say a dicky-bird. I'm going to mention a name and if it's correct, just nod. That's all and we're gone.'

Sarah felt useless, gave Spiro a small smile.

Brant said, 'Tommy Logan.'

For a few moments nothing; Spiro had closed his eyes. Then, a small nod.

Brant said, 'OK, you need anything?'

Head shake.

Brant turned to Sarah, said, 'Let's go.'

87

They were on the ground floor before Sarah got to ask, 'Who's Tommy Logan?'

'A murderin' bastard is who.'

```
Things are entirely
   what they appear
to be and behind them
  there is nothing.
      (Sartre)
```

Falls was shopping. With an air of total abstraction, her eyes kept wandering to the booze counter. The bottles called out, 'Come and get us, ple-eze.'

She sure wanted to. Just crawl into a bottle and shout 'Sayonara, suckers'.

Block out everything.

The Rapist,

Brant,

McDonald,

…And especially Rosie.

But she wasn't certain she'd return. Her father had climbed in and never emerged. Without awareness, she was shredding a head of cabbage. A voice said, 'I don't think it will improve.'

She looked up. A man in his late-forties was smiling at her. He indicated the cabbage, said, 'Like life, it doesn't get better with the peeling away.'

Jeez, she thought, He is one attractive guy.

His hair was snow white and he had a three day beard, which was dark brown. Then the eyes, deeper, holding brown. They held her.

He said, 'According to the experts, shopping is the best way to meet members of the opposite sex.'

She didn't think such gibberish deserved an answer so she said nothing. If it bothered him, he hid it well, said, 'My Mother believed you should go out the door you came in.'

'Which means what, exactly?'

'That I'm backing off; sorry to have interrupted your shredding.' Then he turned and walked off.

Falls said quietly, 'Oh that's great, frighten him right off.'

Her eyes turned again to the booze and she made her decision, shouted, 'Hey!'

He stopped, and when she caught up, she said, 'Tell me more about yer old Mum.'

Brant was going against his instincts but, hell, he felt reckless. As he and Sarah returned to the station, he asked casually, 'What's yer plan for this evening?'

She took it easy, answered, 'I'm going out with friends.'

'Have a good time, eh?'

'I'll try.'

After she'd gone, he sat in the car and tried to figure out what he was feeling. Took out a cigarette and lit it. As the nicotine hit, he tried not to admit that he was disappointed. Then he looked up to see Sarah and McDonald leaving the station.

Her head was thrown back, laughing.

Brant said, 'Fuck.'

Tommy Logan was hyper, roared, 'See what happens to those who fuck with me.'

His men grunted in agreement. What they mainly hoped was he'd be brief.

More: 'Not even the cops can come at us. I had a chief inspector try, eh… Where is he now?

'His DS, the hard case Brant, what had he to offer? Bloody zero, that's what. I'm throwing a party on Friday, the biggest fuckin' bash in south-east London. This is just the beginning.'

Flushed, he wiped his brow and waited for applause. Applause wasn't really in their vocabulary but they knew a response was required. A few hip-hips were produced and it had to suffice. Tommy turned to his right-hand man, said, 'Get the invitations out. Let it be known it's *the* event.'

'Sure, guv.'

He was the only one Tommy trusted. The rest he knew would sell him for a pony.

Ideally, Tommy would have loved to get Johnny Logan singing for the party, but he'd found out he was lost in cabaret in Western Australia. Still, he might do a song himself, it depended on the crowd.

The party invitations went out. Harry, the solicitor's name went on the invites. Thus, a broad cross-section of people could be invited. Including the Super.

The Super rang Harry, 'Harry, it's Superintendent Brown.'

'Superintendent, how are you?'

'Fine, fine. Thank you for the invite.'

'A pleasure. Will you and your lady wife be able to attend?'

'Wouldn't miss it.'

'Splendid, the theme is law and order.'

'Highly commendable.'

'The Lodge will be there.'

'Better and better, Harry. Any help I can give?'

Harry paused, gave it the momentary respect, then, 'Any chance some of your lads might assist with security?'

'They'd be delighted to.'

'Well, that's a load off my mind. See you at the party, then.'

'Absolutely, thanks again.' The call concluded.

Both men felt they'd done pretty damn fine.

Drinking
lights
out

'I don't think I've had piña coladas before.' Sarah had two empty glasses in front of her, working on a third. It was unlikely she'd had a drink of such calibre before.

McDonald knew the barman and had signalled, 'doubles', on each round. What used to be called a Mickey Finn but now was simply referred to as 'loaded'. McDonald was drinking scotch – singles – and watching Sarah go down.

Feeling the alcohol, she said, 'My Mum would forgive a man anything if he was handsome.'

McDonald posed the obvious, 'Would she have forgiven me?'

Sarah gave him a shy look, said, 'You know the answer to that.'

He gave a modest nod which came across as smarmy. She said, 'My father could dance on the side of a saucer.'

She pronounced it 'soo-sir' as the coladas kicked in.

McDonald gave the obligatory chuckle, asked, 'Fancy one for the road?'

Emboldened, she asked, 'One what?'

Music to his ears.

Another drink and it would be Ride City.

Band

'Own Us' were an up and coming band. A cross twixt Oasis and Verve, they were still hungry. Word of mouth was beginning to repeat their name and a record deal was in the air. When approached to do Tommy Logan's party, they didn't hesitate a moment, said, 'No.' Relayed back to Tommy, he said, 'Fuck 'em.'

Then, 'Burn 'em.'

Tommy's right-hand man proposed he have a chat with them. Tommy asked, 'Why, Mick?'

'Cos they'll get us lots of press.'

'OK, have a shot but if nothing's doing, screw 'em.'

'They'll agree, I guarantee it.'

The lead singer was named Matt Wilde (sic). He had acquired the mandatory mid-Atlantic drawl for rock stars. Plus, he scratched a lot. Mick found them rehearsing in a warehouse at the Elephant. He listened to their set and thought, Christ, they're bad.

Matt called a break and signalled to Mick. Being summoned by a nineteen-year-old pup was energising. The star was scratching his neck, asked, 'What's yer bag man?'

'I'd like you to reconsider doing the Law 'n' Order party gig.'

'No can do man, never gonna happen. It hasn't got, like, cred. You hear what I'm saying?'

Mick shrugged, asked, 'Do any Vince Gill?'

'What?'

'You have a mobile?'

'Course.'

'Tell you what, give Kate a buzz.'

'Kate?'

'Is there an echo in here? …Yeah, Kate, yer model girl-friend.'

Matt was less sure of himself, took up his mobile and, as required, dialled. 'Kate?'

'Matthew, hi.'

Mick said, 'Ask her if there's a blue Datsun parked outside.'

He asked… waited, then, 'There is… OK.'

Mick nodded, said, 'There's a bloke sitting here, he's got an acid container… need I paint a picture.'

Matt jumped at him and got an almighty blow to the solar plexus. The band members murmured but didn't move.

Mick said, 'Copyright infringement but we've got it sorted… haven't we, Matt?'

Matt, still on his knees said, 'I'll go to the cops.'

Mick hunkered down beside him, said, 'That would be very silly. Where would Kate get a new face, eh? You have a little think about it.'

Mick stood up, patted Matt's head, said, 'I think coffee break's over.'

'There's no such thing as
unconditional love.
You just find a person
with the same set of
conditions as yourself.'
(Mark Kennedy).

F alls wasn't sure what to wear. She had been through
her wardrobe, rejected it all. He'd said, 'Let's have a
drink, see how we go?'

Out loud she said, 'Meaning, if I don't bore the arse offa
him, we'll move to level two.' And instantly chided
herself.

If she was to get out of the mire, she'd need to change
her attitude. Decided to go down-home-folks, pulled on

tight worn 501's and a UCLA sweatshirt. Pair of red baseball shoes and she was Miss Selfridge.

'What do I call you?' she'd asked.

He thought about it, then, 'Ryan.'

'Like Ryan O'Neal?'

He smiled, 'Not really.'

They'd arranged to meet at The Cricketers. When she arrived he got out of a car, said, 'You're on time.'

'Oh, was it a test?'

He stopped, said, 'You've some mouth on you.' But he was smiling so she let it slide.

Inside, the pub was hopping and he explained, 'Darts night.'

'Oh.'

She'd made a commitment that come what may, she'd tell the truth. Even if he asked what she did. Most times, say you're a cop, they'd say, 'You're never!'

What hung there was not a woman being a cop but a bogey, a *black* woman. Most legged it. So she'd tell the truth, all down the line.

Okay.

He asked, 'To drink?'

'Bacardi and coke.'

Got a table away from the dart players. He came with the drinks, scotch and water chaser, said, 'Cheers.'

'Cheers, Ryan.'

A tight smile as his drink hit, then he asked, 'What do I call you?'

'Yvette.'

First lie.

'Nice, I like it.'

'Do you work?'

'Customer services.'

Second lie.

She crossed her fingers, a third lie was outright wicked so she asked, 'Are you married?'

'That's fairly direct, does it matter?'

'If we're planning an engagement.'

He traced his finger on the rim of the glass, said, 'I'm married with two kids, I'm not planning on leaving her.'

Falls was taken aback. At the very least, he could have whinged that his wife didn't understand him.

She said, 'Yet...'

'What?'

'You're not planning on leaving her *yet*.'

He gave an uncertain smile and she added, 'Give a girl a bit of hope.'

'Oh.'

Jeez, she thought, is he going to be as thick as two planks.

Then he said, 'I don't like lying.'

'You must have an amazing wife... shit, I mean life.'

He finished his drink, grimaced, then: 'I said I don't like it, not that I don't do it.'

The music got louder and Falls asked, 'Like this?'

'Yeah, I do, but I don't know it.'

'It's Ocean Colour Scene.'

'I believe you.'

'Called 'Beautiful Thing' with PP Arnold on there.'

'You like music?'

'C'mon Ryan, what colour am I?'

'Sorry... look Yvette, could you cut me some slack here. I'm nervous and it cuts my banter into shit.'

She felt her heart jump, touched his hand, said, 'Nervous is good.'

Later, they drove up the Edgware Road for bagels and

lox. You have to know someone real well or not at all. Plus, it helps if they like lox. She did.

That night, after they'd made loud, sweaty, exhilarating love, she said, 'Is it just me, or does lox sound slightly obscene?'

Crying time

Falls was bubbling. She bounced into the canteen and wanted to shout, 'Oh yeah!'

She saw Sarah sitting alone. Head down, the picture of misery. Walking over, she said, 'The star's a little dimmed.'

Sarah looked up, said nothing. The skin above her left eye was bruised.

Falls sat, asked, 'What happened?'

'Why, do you care?'

Falls touched her hand, said, 'Wise up, I'm here.'

Sarah mumbled, 'Thanks.'

'Listen, we could do like in *Cagney and Lacey*.'

'Go to the Women's Room?'

'No… cry.'

Falls stood up, went and got some tea and danish. On

102

the way back she put four sugars in the tea, plonked it on the table, said, 'Here.'

'Oh I couldn't.'

'It's for the sugar rush but it won't last, nothing does. You can tell me on the upswing.'

Come the upsurge, came the story.

Like this: 'I was having a drink with… with McDonald. He was getting me piña coladas. I've had them before but not like this. By the time we left, I was near legless. Next thing I know, we're in the front seat of his car and he's trying to push… his… thing in my mouth. I hit my eye against the door and then I vomited all over his… his, lower part. He got so angry, he pushed me outta the car. I was lying on the pavement, and this I do remember, he leaned over to shut the door and said, "Yah useless slag". Then he drove off.

'I dunno how I got home. Can I have some more tea, it was lovely?'

Falls got the tea, then asked, 'What ya going to do?'

'I dunno. Will you tell me?'

Falls took a deep breath, then, 'You could charge him.'

'Oh God.'

'God won't help and neither will the brass. They'll drag you through it and make it impossible to stay in the job. You might – big *might* – make some trouble for him but they'll massacre you.'

Sarah looked set to cry again, said, 'So, he gets away with it?'

Falls grabbed her wrist, said, 'I never said to let it go, I just told you about the official method.'

Hope now in Sarah's eyes, 'There's another way?'

Falls gave a smile that Brant would have understood, said, 'Course there is.'

Once we were werriers

Brant was drinking a sauza sunrise. A close relation of The Eagles' 'Tequila S', it consists of two Shots of Sauza Tequila, and…

lightly carbonated orange juice.

Brant was able to tell this to Roberts with some expertise mainly because the barman had just told him. There's a tapas bar on the corner where Kennington Road hits Kennington Park Road. Brant had arranged to meet Roberts there.

'Why?' asked Roberts.

'Cos I'm feeling Spanish.'

'You are a weird person, sergeant but, why not?'

Brant got there first. A barman in near flamenco gear, said, 'Hi.'

Brant said, '*Buenas Tardes.*'

'*Senor, habla espanol?*'

'Naw, that's it, I do have another word but I'd like to ration it.'

The barman, not sure if this was humour, smiled. He was sure Brant was *el polica*. He'd be *mucho* cautious.

Brant said, 'I dunno all this stuff from shit. What d'ya recommend?' And thus he was enjoying his second.

Later, he told the barman he'd try taco, enchillados, cerveza, if he could stand up.

'*Bueno,*' said a very nervous barkeep. The waitress was in her late ambitious thirties. Her mileage showed but she'd made the best of it. A raw sexuality danced in her eyes. She said to the barman, nodding at Brant, 'Now, there is a bull of a man, a real *el toro.*'

The barman sighed. He was going to apply for income support.

Roberts tasted his drink, said, 'You could get a liking.'

'Good man, that's the spirit.'

Roberts, the only person who ever got to use Brant's first name, said, 'Tom, I hate to worry you but…'

Brant was shaking his head, 'I don't worry.'

Roberts stood back from the bar, said, 'My mistake. You're a warrior, yeah.'

Brant had the grace to look ashamed, said, 'Oh gawd, do I sound like a horse's ass?'

'Yes.'

'OK… What's worrying you?'

'A new sergeant being transferred to us. Starts Monday.'

Brant shrugged. 'I know.'

'Do you? Oh shit, you're still bugging the office.'

'Course… might I add, they dislike me.'

'That's true.'

'I hadn't finished, but they outright hate you.'

'Jesus!'

'Yeah. The new guy's named Porter Nash.'

'All together?'

'And he's a good cop.'

Roberts asked for a beer. The barman got it, said, '*Una Cerveza.*'

Brant lit up. 'Ah, that's beer.'

'It's Don Miguel, *senor, mucho gusto.*'

'Yeah… later Juan.'

Roberts asked, 'Are we gonna eat?'

'Let's get a bit pissed, then we won't care what we eat.'

'That's your plan?'

'For the moment. Anyway Porter Nash ain't going no further than sergeant, despite having a degree in criminology.'

'Christ, you're well informed. What's the matter with Porter Nash?'

Brant smiled. 'His dance card's not full.'

'What?'

'He's a poofter, an arse bandit.'

Roberts took a nervous look round, said, 'Jeez ,sarge, keep it down.'

English graffiti

'They're Spaniards, they hate pillow-biters.'

They went quiet for a while, get some concentrated drink down, then Brant asked, 'Any ideas on how to get Tommy Logan?'

'Nothing feasible yet.'

'We could shoot him.'

'If it were anyone else but you, sergeant, I'd think that was a joke.'

Brant raised his hand, shouted, 'José… food please… *arriba*… don't worry, guv, I got the lingo covered and I think I'll get to ride the waitress.'

❖

Porter Nash was finishing up the Sunday papers. Reading about Peter Ackroyd, he noted:

'There was only the game of living
and the reality of writing.'

'Hmmmph,' he said and substituted 'policing' for
'living' and 'homosexuality' for 'writing'. Not bad but it
would be somewhat awkward to slide into conversation.
The phone rang.

He lifted the receiver, said, 'Yes?'

'Faggots aren't welcome in Kennington.'

Nash said, 'Thanking you for your interest.'

And hung up.

He stood up and stretched. He looked a little like
Michael York with edge. He was tall with blond hair and
that fresh-faced English look that's often mistaken for
weakness. Yet again he wondered why he had asked for a
transfer. It wasn't as if he expected some amazing toler-
ance in the south-east. But he'd been going stale and ceas-
ing to care. Whatever else happened, he wanted to care.

Monday morning when he entered the canteen, it went
completely quiet. Packed to capacity before the week's
mayhem began. He went to the counter and got a tea.
They knew he knew the toilets of both sexes had been
written on… saying:

SERGEANT PORTER NASH
SUCKS ANY DICK

Even the tea lady knew. He avoided her eyes but unlike
most of the ill-mannered buggers in there, he said, 'please'
when he asked for things, and 'thank you' when he got
them.

As he walked away, she said to the cashier. 'Well, say
what you like about him, he has great manners.'

'They do, always.'

He walked back down the length of the canteen, then took a sip of tea, put the cup down. As he headed out, conversation began to buzz but he stopped, turned and said, 'I'm not arguing the basic truth of the toilet graffiti.' And then he raised his voice, 'But I do take exception to the word *any*. Even I draw the line at Sergeant Brant.'

Then he was gone.

A moment later, huge applause erupted. By evening, not a trace of the graffiti remained. Later, when he and Falls had become friends, she asked, 'Did you ever find out who wrote the graffiti?'

'Oh yes.'

'Who?'

'I did it myself.'

Falls would rarely be as impressed again.

Some friendships take a lot of work, others just develop, due to geography and environment. Then, now and again, you get the instant variety.

Even before they got to know each other, the friendship was cemented. Not love at first sight, but out of the same stable. Thus it was for Falls and Porter Nash. A near riot was sizzling in the DSS at the Elephant. Nash and Falls took the call.

Outside the station, he asked, 'You want to drive?'

'You're the rank, I'll follow orders,'

He could see the spirit in her eyes. He said, 'I order myself to drive.' She liked that.

As he drove, he felt her examination, asked, 'See anything you like?'

'I was thinking you got a rough reception.'

'Honest in its way.'

'Is that how you see it?'

'You want me to call them rednecks and bigots?'

'I do.'

He considered, then, 'That's because you're black.'

It hung there till she said, 'As I'm painted.'

'Touché.'

Approaching the DSS, she asked, 'How are you going to tackle this?'

'Badly.'

'Uh-uh, should we ask for back-up?'

'We should get guns but what the hell, let's make it up as we go along.'

They could hear the disturbance and it sounded bad. He said, 'Of course there's always the master plan.'

'Yeah?'

'Run.'

'That's my favourite.'

Nash strode into the middle of the DSS office. Four or five different fights were happening on the left. Staff were cowering behind protective glass. A chair bounced off it. Falls tried to keep up with Nash. He stopped in the centre, roared, *'Who wants money – now?'*

A chorus of:

'What?'

'Eh?'

'Who's 'e then?'

'Wanker!'

He continued: 'Those who want their money, please gather to the right; those wishing to fight, please await the riot police.'

A stocky figure emerged from the crowd, asked, 'Who the fuck are you?'

'I'm the man giving the money.'

People began to move to the right and Nash said to Falls, 'Get the staff moving.'

She did.

The stocky guy marched up to Nash, asked, 'Wotcha gonna do tomorrow?'

'Eh?'

'When I start another fight, will you give me more money.'

'What's your name?'

'Les.'

Nash moved closer, said quietly, 'Can I give you fifty quid?'

'You what?'

'Tomorrow, it won't be my problem but I need to look good today... know what I mean?'

Les considered, then, 'Is that fifty on top of my dole?'

'Of course.'

'OK.'

'Let's step outside, keep it discreet.'

Falls watched the two men leave. They seemed almost friendly. With Les out, the riot fizzled away. The DSS manager approached, said, 'Thank you, it could have turned nasty.'

Falls nodded, and the manager, anxious to please, asked, 'Any suggestion on how to proceed now?'

'Yes, try treating them with a little respect.'

She went to find Nash. He was sitting in the car, no sign of Les.

She asked, 'Where did he go?'

'To pastures greener... or Peckham.'

Then she saw his knuckles were raw and bleeding and he said, 'Hands-on policing.'

'Oh.'

He moved to the passenger seat, asked, 'Will you drive?'

She did.

No words for a while, then she said, 'I have a question.'

'OK.'

'What is it with Barbara Streisand and you lot?'

He laughed out loud, said, 'Only if you answer a question too.'

'Sure.'

'What is it with the baseball caps?'

Making Amends

McDonald was anxious. He'd yet to see Sarah and he was fearful of her reaction.

He wasn't sure if:

A She'd physically attack him,

B She'd verbally attack him,

C A *and* B.

Or, worse, report him.

He was playing these various scenes when she appeared in the corridor and... she was smiling! Jeez, he thought, has she a knife? His experience linked women's smiles to violence.

'Hi,' she said.

'Oh right... listen, about last night... I...' She waved him quiet, said, 'I'm the one who needs to apologise. I blacked out after the pub, you must have taken me home.'

'Ahm… yeah… I did… you don't remember?'

'I am mortified. Please let me make it up to you.'

'What?'

'Dinner at my place, Friday… eight o' clock… do you eat curry?'

'Curry… sure, that's great… I'll bring some wine.'

She gave a shy smile, 'Just mineral water for me. I want to remember this night.'

'Sparkling?'

'I'm lit up already.'

'What about the hotel
where I was asked, do I
want the double bed or the
comfortable bed?
I thought, 'This is a
quiz I am not up to'
(Janet Street-Porter)

Brant stirred, thought, Oh no, not again.
But OK… he wasn't dying. Went to stretch and his
left hand touched a face.
'Jesus!' he roared, sitting straight up.
Took a quick look:
A woman… thank God.
Then he looked again: the Spanish woman.

Yahoo, he'd scored… way to go, Brant!

For one horrible moment a movie flashed through his head. Jane Fonda comes out of a blackout to find a corpse beside her.

If he could just remember her name. Weren't all these Spanish women called the same?

His hangover, though not a killer, was jamming his mental faculties. *Isabella!* Yeah, didn't they even have a queen with the name?

He went to get some tea and clothes. Took another peek at her, not bad at all. Made the tea and dry swallowed aspirin.

Rough.

Got some toast done then took it back to the bedroom. Thought it was a shame to wake her, because then she'd start to talk. Touched her arm, said, 'Isabella?'

No movement.

Poked harder.

'*Que?*'

'*Buenos tardes*, Isabella.'

She took a moment to focus, landed, asked, '*Que es* Isabella… who is this… is evening?'

'No, it's morning.'

She sat up, none of the modest grabbing for sheets.

Let it show.

'You said, *Buenos tardes*.'

'It's kinda all I got.'

She tasted the tea, went, '*Caramba!*'

And leapt out of bed, said, 'This is no good, I'll make us Spanish coffee.'

'But I don't have anything from Spain.'

She put her hands on her hips, asked, 'And what am I?'

'Oh… right.'

She disappeared into the kitchen with a shopping bag. Time on, she's back with coffee and baked or heated toast – sorta. Brant tasted the coffee, said, 'It tastes like… vanilla…'

'*Bueno*, now eat, and then you'll make fiery love to your woman.'

Brant was less sure about the last bit. Mornings were not a passionate time for him. He asked, 'So what, you carry mini meals around with you just in case?'

'It's my shopping and I didn't get home.'

He thought the coffee wasn't half bad. Could vanilla taste bitter? This did.

Took some toast and said, 'I never ate sweet toast, like it's got edge.'

'Now we make love.'

He stood up, time to take charge.

Went and got her a T-shirt, said, 'You go and shower, I've got to go to work.'

She put on the T-shirt and it reached her knees. On its front were the words:

> I am a natural blond
> Please talk slowly

It amused him all over again. He gave her a slap on the arse, said, 'Let's move it, toots.'

As he headed for work, she said, 'My name is Concheta.'

For one bizarre moment, he thought she said, 'Cochise'.

He said nothing and she added, 'Those close to me call me Cheta.'

'OK.'

'Please, one time, say it.'

'What… oh… all right… Cheta.'

'*A muy buena*, you are *mucho simpatico*.'

He looked at his watch, said, 'I'm bloody late is what I am.'

❖

That evening, Brant was saying to Roberts, 'I swear, guv, she stayed the night.'

'I don't believe it.'

'Straight up, guv – and mad for it. Got to go.'

Roberts was impressed and envious, said, 'You always land on yer feet.'

Brant gave his lucky smile, answered, 'Always.'

Outside the station, the rain was lashing down. To Brant's amazement, he saw two white teenagers about to break into his Volvo. If not exactly broad daylight, it was brazen.

'Oi!' he shouted and came running.

Grabbed one by the neck. A long steel bar slipped from the kid's hands, clattered on the kerb. Brant was about to launch forth when an incredible pain wound up his insides, sweat poured down his face.

He dropped to one knee, near doubled in agony.

The first kid asked, 'What's with 'im?'

The other kid, marvelling at their deliverance, said, 'Bugger's sick he is.'

Brant pushed out his left hand to grab the car for support.

The second kid said, 'Jeez, look at the watch, it's a Tag.'

'What?'

'Take the bleeding thing.'

The first kid was dubious, 'Is it a fake?'

Through his pain, Brant tried to say yes but it emerged

118

as a grunt. The second kid moved forward, grabbed Brant's wrist and took the watch, said, 'Let's go… quick.'

Brant lay on the pavement, rain caressing his face.

Brant threw up and that made him a little better. He managed to get to his feet and, after four attempts, he got the door open. Fell in behind the wheel and let his head rest. Every inch of him was soaked. He almost passed out, then came to. Weak as a kitten but better. Put the car in gear and drove slowly home.

He didn't intend reporting this. Him, mugged by kids. He'd lose his rep. The Tag he'd get back, by Christ, see if he didn't. But his rep, he couldn't jeopardise that. Like luck it was near impossible to recapture. At home he fell on the bed, damp clothes an' all and slept for ten hours.

Ice Cream

Roberts, as per deal, bought a copy of the *Big Issue* every week. His vendor knew he was a cop and seemed unfazed. He was eating from a tub of Haagen Dazs ice-cream.

Roberts said, 'Bit cold for it, isn't it?'

The vendor moved aside, said, 'Look.'

Behind him was a large box with maybe another dozen tubs.

Roberts asked, 'You also sell ice-cream?'

The vendor laughed, 'A while ago a Daimler pulled up at the kerb. The window rolls down and a woman said, "You there, come here".'

He mimicked the posh to perfection, continued, 'I thought it was Liz, come to give me an MBE.'

Roberts laughed.

''Ere, I'm serious, guv… they gave one to a traffic warden last year. So, I goes over, took me cap off and this woman, leans out, asks, "Are you one of the homeless chappies?"

'I said, we sell the *Big Issue* for the homeless, yes Ma'am.

'She says, "Righty ho, my driver has something for you people." Then she tapped the glass partition for the driver and shuts the window on me.

'The driver gets out and he's in all the gear, peaked cap and boots. Like a nazi!'

The vendor stopped and sold two copies to two girls and gave them a tub each. They were delighted.

He winked at Roberts, said, 'Like loyalty cards, a little bonus for my regulars. Any road, the nazi opens the boot and takes out the ice-cream. I asked, "What am I supposed to do with that?" He gave me the look, said, "Try eating it".'

The vendor took another taste, said, 'It's not bad if you put a touch o' lager in it.'

Roberts took out his change, had only a fiver… The vendor said, 'We take all the major credit cards.'

Roberts gave him the five, got change, then waited a moment… no tub. Roberts said, 'Well, see you next week.'

Dejected, he was walking away when the vendor shouted, 'Oi, you forgot yer Haagen Dazs.'

'The only actress on the planet who can play a woman whose child has been killed by wild Australian dogs and can actually have you rooting for the dingoes.'
(Joe Queenan on Meryl Streep.)

Falls smiled as she recalled Ryan's reaction to *A Cry In The Dark* when she put on the video.

They'd planned an evening at home, her home, where they'd:

Make love
Eat
Make love
Watch a video.

He cried, 'Oh Jesus, no, not Streep again. C'mon darlin', I watched *Out Of Africa* with you, but I swear, I can't go another session with her.'

They watched *The Untouchables* instead.

She'd been seeing Ryan for two weeks, twice he'd stayed over. On the video nights. Little did he realise, she'd planned on the whole Streep catalogue. Most days she felt:

Queasy
Exhilarated
Nervous
Giddy
Had no appetite
Phone fixated.

And realising, said, 'Oh shit, I love him.'

She was acting like a schoolgirl, trying out his name, projecting babies, wanting to talk about him incessantly. Tried to burst her own balloon with:

He's married,
Kids,
Said he won't leave.

But no, that balloon of hope just climbed on up there.

He'd said, 'You look good in red.' Changed her whole wardrobe. Oh yeah.

She turned on the telly, got local news, *London Tonight*. The top story was:

RETURN OF THE CLAPHAM RAPIST

She felt dizzy. Another attack had taken place, the

details were the same: a black woman, a knife, an alley-way.

'It can't be!' she cried.

A local councillor followed demanding an inquiry into police methods. And then he asked, 'Who was the man killed in a police decoy operation?'

The phone rang. She picked it up, heard, 'You and McDonald in the Super's office at nine sharp.'

'Yes, sir.'

She rang Brant. He sounded groggy and she told him the news. He didn't reply for a moment, then, 'It's a copy-cat.'

'But what about the guy who attacked me?'

Deep intake of breath and he snarled back, 'When a guy jumps you in a dark alley, and puts a knife to yer throat, he's up to no good, believe me.'

'But maybe he wasn't *the* Clapham Rapist.'

'Well he was some bloody area's rapist and good friggin' riddance.'

He slammed down the phone. She started to cry… wanted to drink, then rang Ryan.

He answered, 'Yeah?'

'Help me.'

'I'm on my way.'

She tried to compose herself. Decided she'd only tell him a little.

When he arrived, he put his arms round her and she told him the lot. He'd made her a cup of sweet tea and held it while she drank. When she'd finished her story, he said, 'I'd never have took you for a copper.'

'Because I'm black.'

'Cos you're beautiful.'

Fright night

Neville Smith was doing good. A stockbroker, he had a house in Dulwich, two kids at boarding school, and his new car. An Audi. As he gazed at it he said, '*Vorsprung Techniquo.*'

It was that and more.

Neville liked to drive fast and just a tad recklessly. He truly believed that ninety percent of drivers had no right to be there. They all had the look of National Assistance. He liked to cut them up and take the road. Austin Micras, Ka's, Datsuns, 'all garbage,' he said.

There'd been a diversion so he found himself heading for the Elephant roundabout. If he could make the light, he'd gain time. He swerved in front of a Rover almost touching the fender. He definitely took paint and made the light. He could see the driver and his passenger shouting at him. The adrenalin rush made him near euphoric and he put up the two fingers.

Through the lights and he accelerated, shouted, 'Morons!'

The Rover pulled in near the park and Tommy Logan asked, 'You got the number?'

'Sure did, guv.'

'Good man, I want to know who he is by lunchtime.'

The driver was speed dialling, said, 'I'm on it.'

Two days later, Neville was relaxing over a gin and tonic. His wife asked, 'How about sushi?'

He took his cue, followed with the expected line, 'If you knew sushi like I know sushi...'

They both laughed, not so much humour as the ease of familiarity.

'Will you open the wine darling while I prepare the table?'

'Of course.'

He'd done that and was about to glance at the news when the door bell rang.

He said, 'I'll go.'

Opening the door, he saw two heavy set men. One asked, 'Do you own an Audi?' And gave the registration.

'Yes I do... why?'

The first said, 'You've got dirt on the side.'

'What?'

Then he was pushed backwards and the men followed him in closing the door. The first man began to slap Neville across the face. His wife came running, started to scream.

Tommy Logan kicked her in the stomach, said, 'Don't start.'

126

Now Tommy moved over to Neville and spun him round, face down on the stairs. Tore Neville's pants down and said, 'Do yah want it, eh? Want some of this?'

Tommy stood back, asked, 'Have I got yer attention?'

'Yes.'

'Do you know who I am?'

'No.'

Tommy lashed out with his fist, roaring 'I'm the guy you cut up in traffic.'

Another blow and, 'And gave the two fingers to.'

'Oh God, I'm sorry.'

'You're sorry now, sorry we caught you.'

Neville was blubbering, 'Let me make it up to you… money…'

'Shaddup!' Tommy said. And, as if he'd just thought of it, 'Course, the car's to blame.'

Neville, sensing a tiny shimmer of hope, said, 'You're right… one gets carried away.'

Tommy smiled said, 'It must be punished… bad car.'

Tommy pushed Neville out to the garage.

Took a look round then said, 'My man has just the ticket.'

Mick came in, dragging the woman and carrying a hurley, handed it to Tommy, who took it and gave a slow swing. Asked, 'Isn't it a beauty?'

Handed the hurley to Neville, said, 'Go on… won't bite you.'

For a moment, as he held it, a fire touched his eyes.

Tommy laughed, 'Don't even think about it or I'll make you eat it.'

'What do you want me to do?'

'Punish the car, beat the living daylights outta it and keep saying "bad car".'

Tommy looked over at Neville's wife, said, 'If you don't, my man there is going to fuck her all over this garage. Trust me, he's an animal.'

Neville lifted the hurley, said, 'Bad car.'

Say cheese

Brant was sitting in his armchair, smoking and thinking. In his career, he'd broken two major cases with a hunch. He'd acted on them when all the evidence pointed elsewhere. He'd play what he knew, then let it settle, add in the possibilities and bingo, he'd get an answer.

Now he sat bolt upright in his chair, said, 'Jesus.' Then he got on the phone, said, 'It's Brant.'

'Sergeant, how are you? Did the bugging device work?'

'Like a dream.'

'Good, do you need something?'

'A hidden camera.'

'No problem, where is it to go?'

'In a kitchen.'

'Mmm, tricky to install.'

'It's my own kitchen.'

'Right... when?'

'Now.'

'Gimme yer address, I'll be there in an hour.'

Brant gave it, said, 'I appreciate it.'

'A pleasure.'

'I'll watch for you.'

The man laughed, said, 'Sergeant, leave the surveillance to us, it's what we do.'

❖

That evening when Cheta arrived, she was carrying bags of groceries. First off she gave him a swallowing kiss, then pushed him off, with '*Hombre*... my *caballero*, first we eat.'

Needling, he said, 'Let's go out.'

No way. She indicated the bags of stuff.

'This is especial, now... you relax, the kitchen is mine... no *hombres* allowed.'

He made as if to follow, 'That's not very liberated.'

She threw her hands, mock horror, said, 'I am Spanish.'

'OK... what's on the menu?'

'Paella... with the recipe of Andalucia, *gorelax*.'

He opened a beer but barely touched it, gave her forty-five minutes, then, 'Honey, I've got to go.'

She came storming out, 'How? I hear no phone.'

'My mobile, very discreet but it's urgent.'

'But the dinner... is ready... have *pocito*, taste.'

He was already at the door, 'I'll make it up to you tomorrow.'

'Will I wait?'

'No, it's an all nighter.'

He waited outside in the Volvo. He figured she was cunning but none too smart. They rarely got to be both.

After half-an-hour, a cab pulled up, she came out, gave her destination, never looked round. She lived in Streatham, back of the swimming pool. A row of terraces in the passageway, she went into the second.

As he drove away, he phoned Roberts, asked, 'Like to see a video?'

'What now?'

'It's a one-off, you'll recognise the star.'

'Do I bring anything.'

'Handcuffs, probably.'

The picture was quality, none of that grainy effect. If Brant thought it was strange to watch her in his own kitchen, he didn't show it. Just smoked a lot of Weights. They could see her put the paella on the plates then go to her bag, extract a small bottle and douse one plate.

Brant said, 'Guess who that's for.'

Then she was gone.

Brant explained, 'It's me telling her I'm off.'

Back she came and they could see her rage as she scraped the dishes into the bin.

Roberts asked, 'You have the bin?'

'Oh yeah.'

Next she tidied up, washed all the gear, even wiped the floor. Roberts said, 'Good little housekeeper though.'

Brant smiled, answered, 'Deadly.'

The lab test showed liquid arsenic.

Roberts asked, 'Wanna come when we give her a tug?'

'No… I'll pass I think.'

Later, Roberts said, 'Buy you a drink?'

'Yeah great, but a pub with no barmaids.'

'Right.'

131

After they'd had a few, Roberts asked, 'Wanna hear about it?'

'Sure.'

'She had a reason.'

'Oh good, that makes it all right then.'

Roberts signalled for another round, said, 'She claims she never intended to kill, just to sicken you as it is men always sickened her.'

Brant took a belt of scotch, said, 'A nutter eh?'

'Barking.'

Roberts felt he should offer some support or even solace. But, all he could give was, 'Don't let it put you off women.'

Brant gave a huge belch, said, 'It sure as hell put me off paella.'

Benediction moon

'I'm a spiritual person' the man said to Porter Nash. It was a rite of passage at any new station, you got the loopy cases. This was certainly that.

The man had been attacked by a pimp and a hooker. They'd given him a sound thrashing. Nash asked, 'How did you happen to ah… meet these people?'

The man sighed, he didn't suffer fools gladly.

'I go to professional ladies and to demonstrate their baseness to them, I pay them in a similar coinage.'

'You're not a priest, are you?'

Tolerant smile, 'I'm a deacon of the flesh.'

Nash read the charge sheet again. He was getting a migraine. He said, 'You gave the *lady* two forged fifties.'

'It's debauchery, paid for by deceit.'

Nash asked, 'Where do you get the funny money?'

133

'A chap in an ale house had a bag of them, a British Homes Store brand… yes, I'm sure of that.'

Nash said, 'You'll go down for… something.'

The man stood up, 'I'll embrace the penitentiary.'

'Believe me, they'll help you.'

As they took him away, he shouted, 'I see auras.'

'Course you do.'

'And yours, sir, is blue.'

Nash had to ask, 'That good?'

''Ish.'

He went to the canteen and the tea lady was delighted anew with his manners. Ordered tea and got two slices of toast he hadn't ordered, said, 'I didn't order toast.'

She gave a full silver toothed smile, 'It's my little treat.'

'Gosh… how wonderful.'

Thinking, if he got five minutes with a novel, he'd better meet the day. Had a round of toast drenched and dripping in butter, then opened his book.

'Can I join you?'

Falls.

He thought, Ah, shag off, is it too much to ask for a few minutes?

He said, 'Please do.'

She asked, 'Wotcha reading?'

'It's Jane Smiley's *A Thousand Acres*'.

'I dunno her.'

He wanted to roar, 'Quelle surprise!', but said, 'She won the Pulitzer.'

'That's good?'

'It's not bad.'

'Is it good?'

'Well, I'm only on the third acre but it's boring the pants off me.'

She laughed, said, 'Thanks for not treating me like an ignoramus.'

He offered the toast, saying, 'It's heaven.'

She took it, asked, 'How'd you get toast like this?'

He only smiled, so she said, 'I think we're mates.'

Nod.

'So, can I ask your opinion.'

He gave her the final slice, a true sacrifice and said, 'I'm a good choice cos I tell people what they want to hear.'

'Oh God, don't do that.'

'OK.'

'There's a man…'

'I hear you.'

She glanced around, she sure as hell didn't want anyone to hear, asked, 'How do I know if it's… you know… love?'

This Nash could do. He smiled said, 'A few questions will answer that.'

'Oh.'

'Do you wanna go for it?'

'Ahm… OK, I think.'

'Do you think of him [here Nash did an American accent] like all the time?'

'Yes.'

'Have you got the runs?'

She laughed and nodded. 'Is your appetite screwed? Do songs seem to be directed specifically at you? Do you want to do nothing but stare out the window?'

'Yes, yes, yes.'

'Now for the biggie, the litmus test.'

Falls felt nervous, said, 'I feel nervous.'

'So you should, here goes.'

He went American again.

'Would you, like, just *die* if you saw him with somebody else?'

'Oh yes.'

'Then I must inform you, WPC Falls, that you are completely and irrevocably in love, and may God have mercy on your soul.'

Later, rearranging his CDs, he pulled out 'Benediction Moon'. Its mix of keening loss, awareness, and wonder were the articulation of a heart on fire.

Let's party

A warehouse near The Elephant had been trans-formed. A crowd had gathered outside to see the party-goers arrive. When Tommy Logan got there he gave two fingers to the crowd. That they under-stood. Gave him a rousing cheer. 'My people' he said.

As fixed, security was provided by off duty cops. McDonald was on the door, he said to Tommy: 'Good evening, sir.'

Tommy palmed him a ten, said, 'Keep up the good work.'

Inside the band were tuning up. Tommy said to Mick, 'Who are they?'

'The band you requested.'

'Can they play?'

'They're a spit from being famous, guv.'

The warehouse had lived many lives. At one stage it had been a cinema and a balcony ran along the back. The projection room was still intact. A flight of stairs led from it to the street. Mick moved up to the band, said to the surly Matt, 'Get started.'

'We're artists man, we don't just *start*.'

Mick hopped lightly on to the stage, went nose-to-nose, said, 'You're history if you don't and never, like fuckin' *never* call me *man*, get it?'

He got it.

They kicked off with a cover of The Verve's 'Bittersweet Symphony', the extended one.

Tommy said, 'Sounds like the Rolling Stones.'

Mick was clued, said, 'Based on "The Last Time"!'

'It's good, they're OK.'

Mick said, 'They're keen as mustard, chuffed to play for you.'

A stir at the door as the Super arrived. Harry the solicitor behind. Their wives were interchangeable. Like models of Mrs Thatcher. Tommy moved to greet them, signalling to a waiter for champagne. Outside, to the left of the crowd, Brant was leaning on his car, cigarette going. Roberts drove up, rolled down his window, said, 'You're not supposed to be here.'

'You neither.'

'You going to gatecrash?'

'If you're game.'

Roberts smiled, said, 'Lemme park, I'll get back to you.'

Brant flicked the cig away, said, 'I'll be here.'

When McDonald saw them approach, he went, 'Oh, shit.'

Worse, they were smiling at him. Inside, the band were attempting 'Working Class Hero' as a touch of contempt.

But as usual, those who least understood the song were the ones who most appreciated it. Roberts said, 'Bit of moonlighting, McDonald?'

'Sir.'

They made to enter and he stepped in front of them, said, 'Guv, I'll have to see yer invites.'

Brant said, 'Gee, we left them in the car.'

McDonald didn't move and Roberts said, 'S'cuse me son.'

He moved.

The first person they met was Tommy's wife, Tina. She said, 'I can't believe you got invited.'

Roberts looked at her, said, 'Wouldn't miss it for the world.'

The Super glared at them across the hall. Brant waved. More people arrived and the place was becoming crowded. Brant asked Tina to dance, she said, 'Get real.'

Tommy said to Mick, 'I want them outta here.'

'There'd be a scene.'

'Are you saying let 'em be?'

'For now.'

'Fuckers!'

Food was served and Brant was first in line. Got double helpings. His plate overflowing, he moved back to Roberts, said, 'The grub is good, guv, wanna try some?'

Roberts looked at it in disgust, said, 'It would choke me.'

'Food dunno from shit, guv… it's like money.'

'You're getting very philosophical.'

'Naw, just hungry.'

Like all shindigs worth the name, there was a raffle. Cops

love them. Brant had a fistful of tickets, said to Roberts, 'Do you feel lucky?'

'Gimme a break!' And he moved off.

First prize of a music centre went to Harry the solicitor. Good humoured shouts of *Fix! Fix!* punctuated his acceptance of the prize. Tommy was doing the presentation. His face was shining, his triumph assured. He said, 'Second prize of my own personal favourite, a Waterford crystal bowl, goes to a green ticket Number 93.'

When he saw who'd won, his face dropped. Brant. When Brant got to the stage, he gave Tommy a huge hug, whispered, 'Ya wanker.' Then stepped back as Tommy handed over the prize.

Brant took it, looked down at the crowd, then let go. The crystal shattered in a thousand pieces. Brant said, 'Oops!'

On Brant's way down the hall, he came face to face with The Super who said, 'My office, nine of clock sharp.'

Brant smiled, said, 'Wouldn't miss it for the world.'

The band launched into a frenzied version of 'Let's Dance'.

Brant spotted Tina, asked, 'Wanna quickstep?'

'You've got to be kidding.'

'Yeah, you're too fat for it all right.'

Tommy was checking his speech. Before the party finished, he'd say a few words.

He said to Mick, 'There's no jokes, it needs humour.' Mick thought, You're the fuckin' joke, but said, 'Maybe it's best to play it straight.'

'You think?'

'Yeah, more dignity, know what I mean?'

140

'I can do dignified.'

When the time came, all the lights went out. A lone spotlight lit the stage. Tommy strode out. Looking down the hall, he was blinded and could see nowt. He began, 'Officers and ladies…'

A single shot rang and a small hole appeared over his right eye.

He gave a tiny 'Ah,' and fell backward.

Who shot TL?

The suspects were:
Brant
Roberts
Tina Logan
gang rival(s).

Brant and Roberts had received a bollocking from the Super and he let them know they were high on the suspect list. Now, over coffee, Brant said, 'Well, guv, I know I didn't shoot him, did you?'

'No… but I'm shedding no tears.'

'Who do you think?'

'I strongly suspect you.'

Brant laughed. 'What about Tina, his wife?'

'She could have got somebody to do it. Who'd blame her. He sure needed shooting.'

Brant stretched, said, 'It was a great party, I really enjoyed it.'

'God forbid you shouldn't be happy.'

The desk sergeant appeared, said, 'Brant, there's a call for you, a Paul Johnson.'

'I'm not here.'

'He says it's urgent.'

'Tough.'

The sergeant went away muttering.

Roberts asked, 'Who's Paul Johnson?'

'My ex-wife's husband.'

'Oh!'

'Oh is bloody right.'

McDonald was in the Super's office. No Masonic hand-shit this trip. It was ball-busting and vehement.

The Super said, 'For heaven's sake, you were on the door and you didn't see the shooter?'

'It was pandemonium, sir. People were panicked and stampeding. Plus, there's a fire escape leading from the projection booth to the street.'

'The papers are having a field day. We've got to find the shooter and fast.'

McDonald had thought it over and decided to go for broke, said, 'I think I know who it is.'

'What? Spit it out man.'

'DS Brant, sir.'

The Super's eyes bulged.

'Are you mad?'

'Sir, he'd do anything for DI Roberts. He was there and he is without conscience. It has to be him.'

'Can you prove it.'

'I will, sir. I guarantee it.'

Now he was way out on a limb. If he was wrong, he'd be out on his ass.

The Super said, 'OK, keep it under your hat. I don't need to spell it out if you're right *or* if Brant gets wind of your claim.'

'I'll be discreet, sir.'

'You better be.'

Outside the office, McDonald wiped his brow. Sarah was coming along the corridor, asked, 'Are we set for this evening?'

'What?'

'My place, I'm cooking dinner for you.'

'Oh yeah… right… sure.'

He thought 'a leg over' was exactly what he needed. Calm him down and let him focus on frying Brant's ass.

Falls was in the canteen, listening to the various stories on the party. People were poring over the tabloids. Falls asked, 'Can I see the paper?'

One came sailing over to land on the table. The front page had a large photo of Tommy Logan, stretched on the stage. A man was bending over him and there was something about the tilt of his head. She muttered, 'Oh no'.

She got up, ran from the canteen, the paper in her hand. Near collided with Roberts who said, 'Whoa, where's the fire?'

She pushed the paper at Roberts, cried, 'Who's that?'

'Tommy Logan – the late Tommy Logan.'

She tried to control her hysteria, said, 'Not him, the other one.'

'That's Mick Ryan, his lieutenant, the next in line.'

144

'Ryan?'

'Yes, do you know him.'

She gazed at the paper before answering, 'No, no, I don't know him at all.'

When McDonald knocked on Sarah's door, he was carrying flowers and chocolates. On heat, he was anticipating the ride of his life. That she was a snotty little cow only fuelled his excitement. She opened the door, wearing a white silk kimono. Her breasts were tantalisingly on display. He moved inside, pushed her against the wall, began to grope. A few minutes and he'd have popped.

Pushing him away, she said, 'Let's whet out appetites.'

A glass of whiskey was already poured. She asked, 'Is Glenfiddich OK?'

'Aye, lass.'

Truth to tell, he'd never had it. So if it tasted a tad off, he wouldn't know. Put mustiness down to quality.

'You sit here.' And she manoeuvred him into an armchair.

'More?' she asked, coming with the bottle. As he held out his glass, he had to loosen his shirt, said, 'Jeez, it's hot in here.'

She smiled, poured, said, 'Animal heat.'

The room was tilting and he thought, 'I'm legless, how can I be so pissed.'

As he sank back into the armchair, he tried to focus on Sarah but he was seeing double. Odd thing was, he could have sworn that half of Sarah was Falls. What? He closed his eyes.

The doctor said, 'I don't quite know how you managed it but your penis is super-glued to your testicles.'

McDonald didn't know what to say. He wanted to howl. He'd come to in his car with a bastard of a headache. Nothing of the evening could he remember. Bursting for a piss, he found his dick wouldn't budge. Thus the doctor and his absolute mortification.

He strongly suspected the doctor was smirking. Worse, he had a nurse who was outright laughing. The doctor said, 'Here's what we'll do to… ahm… release you, but I won't lie, it's going to be painful.'

It was.

McDonald howled for all he was worth.

Smoking

Brant was standing outside the station with Roberts. He was lighting one cigarette with the stub of another. Roberts said, 'Those will kill you.'

Brant nodded but didn't speak. A young constable came down the steps, said, 'Sarge, there's a call for you.'

'Who is it?'

'Ahm, oh yeah, Paul Johnson.'

'I'm not here.'

'What.'

'Are yah deaf, I'm not available.'

'Oh… right.'

A car pulled up at the kerb and Porter Nash got out. Both men watched him closely. He came right up to Brant, said, 'I have something for you.'

'For me?'

'I caught two teenagers breaking into a car yesterday. They offered me a watch to let them slide.'

Here, Nash put his hand in his pocket, produced the Tag, continued, 'I persuaded them to tell me where they got it.' Brant looked at Nash and the moment hung. Then Nash said, 'Seems they saw you drop it.'

Brant let out a deep breath, took the watch, said, 'I owe you one.'

'Glad to help.'

After Nash had gone, Roberts asked, 'What just happened?' But Brant was raging, spat 'I fuckin' hate that.'

'What?'

'Him. You know, owing him a favour.'

'I thought you'd be glad to get the Tag.'

'They never forget, you know.'

'Who?'

'Queers... they hold it over you...'

Roberts sighed, said, 'You are a very twisted man... very.'

❖

Mick Ryan knocked on Falls door. She opened it, said, 'What do you want?'

'To talk.'

'I'm surprised you have time, I mean aren't you supposed to be running a crime empire.'

He looked round, said, 'Please.'

She had been expecting a rage of homicidal proportions. But all she felt now was sad and tired, said, 'Come in.'

For a moment they simply watched each other. He tried, 'I dunno where to begin.'

'The truth would be nice.'

'I'm not going to apologise for who I am. But I'm truly sorry if you've been hurt.'

'If!'

'I'm getting out… like all the rest, I'll go to the Costa.'

'How nice.'

'Come with me.'

She gave a bitter laugh, asked, 'As what, yer au pair?'

'You can have your own villa… it could work.'

Falls sat down, said, 'I'm in deep shit over the rapist and you're offering me a shag in Spain. No thanks.'

Ryan went to touch her but let his hand fall away, said, 'Watch the papers on Saturday, it's the least I can do.'

'Oh, you've sold your story.'

He moved to the door, said, 'Take care.'

She said nothing at all.

❖

Brant was heading for the pub, asked Roberts, 'Wanna pint, guv?'

'Naw, I'm knackered.'

The Cricketers was quiet and Brant ordered a Stella. He was getting on the good side of that when a man came into the bar, looked around and headed his way.

He said, 'DS Brant?'

Brant gave the man a hard look, asked, 'Why?'

'I went to the station and they said I might find you here.'

'Helpful bastards, aren't they?'

The man put out his hand, said, 'I'm Paul Johnson.'

Brant ignored the hand, said, 'And that's supposed to tell me what?'

'I'm married to your ex-wife.'

'Oh.'

'I wanted to thank you for extricating me from the shop-lifting charge.'

Brant turned away. 'No big deal, you needn't have wasted the trip.'

But the man didn't go and Brant let his testiness show, barked, 'What?'

'I think I can help you.'

'Help me? And how the fuck could you help me?'

'The Tommy Logan killing. I know who did it.'

Brant moved off his stool, took the man's arm, said, 'Let's park it at the back.'

Moved to a table at the rear, Brant said, 'Let's hear it.'

'A few weeks back, a man named Neville Smith cut up Tommy Logan in traffic. Later, Logan came to Smith's house, terrorised him and his wife. Then, to complete the humiliation, Tommy Logan invited them to his party. Neville Smith is ex-army and a very proud man. His wife told Mary…'

Brant wasn't sure what to say, tried a gruff, 'Thanks.'

It had to suffice. That evening Brant rang Roberts, laid out the story. Roberts listened without comment and Brant asked, 'What will you do, guv?'

'Nothing.'

'Gets my vote.'

Two days later, Roberts got a package in the mail. No note or message, just a cassette tape. He read the title with a tight smile – *Smokie's Greatest Hits*.

When Falls woke late on the Saturday morning, she went

to get the paper before anything else. It was on Page four, a half column:

'Man found naked and chained to a tree on Clapham Common. A notice round his neck read: 'I AM THE COPYCAT RAPIST'. Police were issuing no statement until a full investigation could be launched.'

Falls looked up into a clear blue sky. Saw the trail of a plane, and didn't expect it was heading for the Costa... But... you never could tell.

KEN BRUEN

The Hackman Blues

ISBN 1899344 22 5 — C-format paperback original, £7

"If Martin Amis was writing crime novels, this is what he would hope to write." — Books in Ireland

"…I haven't taken my medication for the past week. If I couldn't go a few days without the lithium, I was in deep shit. I'd gotten the job ten days earlier and it entailed a whack of pub-crawling. Booze and medication is the worst of songs. Sing that!

A job of pure simplicity. Find a white girl in Brixton. Piece of cake. What I should have done is doubled my medication and lit a candle to St Jude — maybe a lot of candles."

Add to the mixture a lethal ex-con, an Irish builder obsessed with Gene Hackman, the biggest funeral Brixton has ever seen, and what you get is the Blues like they've never been sung before. Ken Bruen's powerful second novel is a gritty and grainy mix of crime noir and Urban Blues that greets you like a mugger stays with you like a razor scar.

A White Arrest

ISBN 1899344 41 1 — paperback original, £6.50

The first part of the White Trilogy: "A White Arrest reads like it was written on speed, in one crazed all night burst. It's a thick-eared Police Procedural, frantic with incident. Bit of sex, lot of violence, first in a trilogy. Fun, fast-food fiction."   The List (Galway)

"When it comes to fast, furious, hard-assed crime writing, Ken Bruen is in a class of his own." Time Out

Taming The Alien

ISBN 1899344 49 7 — paperback original, £7.50

The second part of the White Trilogy:

"The grit factor is turned up to its ultimate notch."   The Guardian

"The follow-up to Bizarre fave A White Arrest sees bad cops Brant and Roberts and unlucky WPC Falls up to even more outrageous behaviour. This time the action spreads out of South London and into Galway, New York and San Francisco, as Brixton wideboy 'The Alien' goes on a trans-Atlantic killing spree and big bad Brant just has to follow. Meanwhile, beleaguered Roberts is suffering from skin cancer and Falls gets on the wrong side of a Croydon arsonist. The blackest humour around."   Bizarre

JOHN B SPENCER

Stitch by John B Spencer
ISBN 1 899344 50 0 — paperback original, £7.50

Honour among thieves? You must be joking. Bobby Boy is a career criminal and he's losing it... only he doesn't have a lot left to lose. Just a wife and his self-respect. And he's not letting go of either without a fight. Unreconstructed psychopath Winston Capaldi has stitched Bobby Boy on a sweet deal and Bobby Boy is prepared to take it all the way. Winston, meanwhile, is hunting down the mother who deserted him back in the 'swinging' '60s. And when he finds her, it's not a big hug he has in mind.

"Stitch is a superb book, full of wit, humour and insight into the human condition. Recommended, but not for the easily shocked." — Crime Time   'A fantastic read" — Shots

Tooth & Nail by John B Spencer
ISBN 1 899344 31 4 — paperback original, £7

A dark, Rackmanesque tale of avarice and malice-aforethought from one of Britain's most exciting and accomplished writers. "Spencer offers yet another demonstration that our crime writers can hold their own with the best of their American counterparts when it comes to snappy dialogue and criminal energy. Recommended." — Time Out

Perhaps She'll Die! by John B Spencer
ISBN 1 899344 14 4 — paperback original, £5.99

Giles could never say 'no' to a woman... any woman. But when he tangled with Celeste, he made a mistake... A bad mistake.

Celeste was married to Harry, and Harry walked a dark side of the street that Giles — with his comfortable lifestyle and fashionable media job — could only imagine in his worst nightmares. And when Harry got involved in nightmares, people had a habit of getting hurt. Set against the boom and gloom of eighties Britain, Perhaps She'll Die! is classic noir with a centre as hard as toughened diamond.

Quake City by John B Spencer
ISBN 1 899344 02 0 — paperback original, £5.99

The third novel to feature Charley Case, the hard-boiled investigator of a future that follows the 'Big One of Ninety-Seven' — the quake that literally rips California apart and makes LA an Island. "Classic Chandleresque private eye tale, jazzed up by being set in the future... but some things never change — PI Charley Case still has trouble with women and a trusty bottle of bourbon is always at hand. An entertaining addition to the private eye canon." — Mail on Sunday

The Do-Not Press
Fiercely Independent Publishing

Keep in touch with what's happening at the cutting edge of independent British publishing.

Join The Do-Not Press Information Service and receive advance information of all our new titles, as well as news of events and launches in your area, and the occasional free gift and special offer.

Simply send your name and address to:
The Do-Not Press (Dept. McD)
16 The Woodlands
London
SE13 6TY
or email us: thedonotpress@zoo.co.uk

There is no obligation to purchase and no sales-person will call.

Visit our regularly-updated web site:

http://www.thedonotpress.co.uk

Mail Order
All our titles are available from good bookshops, or (in case of difficulty) direct from The Do-Not Press at the address above. There is no charge for post and packing.
(NB: A post-person may call.)